"You look good enough to eat."

Ryan grinned as his eyes moved from the top of Brandy's blond head over slender curves, slowly down her long, tanned legs to brightly polished pink toenails.

Brandy felt herself melting and knew it had nothing to do with the warmth of the day. "Er, how about breakfast instead?"

He moved within inches of her quivering body, and Brandy felt her temperature shoot up another degree. "Do I have a choice?"

"Of course," she managed, visions of waffles and hotcakes floating through her dazed mind.

Ryan groaned and pulled her against his hard strength. "Then I know what I'm hungry for...."

THE AUTHOR

JoAnn Ross claims the romance-writer heroine of *Duskfire* "is pure fiction." There are no parallels to her own life, she says with a wink. But it's ironic that both JoAnn and Brandy are wonderful storytellers.

Brandy and Ryan's book *Risky Pleasure* will be published as an Intrigue this month. The real author is JoAnn, of course, who had a great time writing the spin-off. JoAnn's been published under her own name as well as under the pseudonyms JoAnn Robb and JoAnn Robbins.

Books by JoAnn Ross
HARLEQUIN TEMPTATION
42—STORMY COURTSHIP
67—LOVE THY NEIGHBOR
77—DUSKFIRE

Duskfire

JoANN ROSS

HarlequinBooks

TORONTO • NEW YORK • LONDON
AMSTERDAM • PARIS • SYDNEY • HAMBURG
STOCKHOLM • ATHENS • TOKYO • MILAN

To Jay with love

Published October 1985

ISBN 0-373-25177-7

Printed in Canada

1

"'THE WAY I FIGURE IT, you gotta treat dames a lot like mushrooms. You know—keep them in the dark and feed them regular doses of steer manure.' For heaven's sake, Maggie, do you honestly expect me to collaborate with any man who'd write such trash?"

Brandy Raines ran out of telephone cord, her pacing brought to an abrupt halt. She slumped into a wicker chair, extending her bare legs in front of her.

"I can't believe I paid two-fifty for this junk."

"Now, Brandy," the feminine voice over the wire coaxed, "you're not giving him a fair trial. Ryan Sinclair has made a fortune with his Johnny Steele series. He's the perfect writer to help you inject a little action into your romances. Honestly, honey, if I didn't think you two would make a great team, I wouldn't have suggested the idea in the first place."

"Oh sure, action." Brandy braced the telephone against an uplifted shoulder as she thumbed through the paperback detective novel. "Listen to this: 'Hymie the Ferret was the kind of snitch who'd sell his grandmother for a fin and blow it all on a nag in the fifth at Santa Anita. It was my rotten luck to show up in time to watch his swan dive off the roof. When Hymie splattered on the pavement like a ripe crenshaw melon, I knew he wouldn't be talking much today...'

"Maggie! How could you do this to me?"

"I haven't done anything but suggest you and Ryan get together and consider collaborating on a romantic suspense novel," the feminine voice soothed expertly. "You write marvelous romances, honey, filled with elegant people falling in love amid cascading flowers and streaming stardust. Ryan, on the other hand, writes fast-moving stories about more earthy individuals. You should complement each other perfectly."

Brandy slammed the book shut, eyeing the front cover as though it were something that had just crawled from underneath a particularly slimy rock. A nude female was lying facedown in a bright red pool of blood, the gun by her side trailing a thin wisp of blue smoke.

"It's amazing just how often these earthy individuals end up naked," she observed dryly, recalling the many times Johnny Steele had ended up in someone's bed. All in the line of duty, of course.

"Don't get snooty, honey," her agent advised. "Remember, Ryan is merely supplying male fantasies. It's not so different from the love scenes you weave into your stories."

"Humph." Brandy expelled a snort as she twisted a long strand of dark honey blond hair around a finger. She had a sneaking suspicion that Johnny Steele was only living out Ryan Sinclair's tacky male fantasies.

"This stuff is at the opposite end of the spectrum from anything resembling love," she argued. "Listen: 'Trixie was warming up like a firecracker on the Fourth of July. The last guy to make it with this dame ended up on a slab in the morgue with a tag on his big toe. But what the hell, I figured, knocking off the last of the gin, a doll like Trixie would probably make it seem worthwhile....' Maggie!"

It was a wail. If there was one thing the two hundred pages of *The Uninvited Corpse* had shown Brandy, it was that she and Ryan Sinclair would never be able to work together. The man obviously had all the sensitivity of a cockroach.

"Just talk to him," Maggie continued to coax. "No one's going to tie you to the railroad tracks until you agree to write with the man, honey. But keep an open mind. While Ryan's books have sold like hotcakes, I'd like him to expand his market. He's going to need help with the female point of view if he's to break into the romance field, Brandy. You'd be doing me a big favor. Just meet him and see what you think."

"All right, Maggie." Brandy sighed her acquiescence wearily. "But only because you're a good friend. Now I'm not promising anything. So don't get his hopes up."

"Thanks, hon. Who knows, you might like the guy, after all."

"That'd be the day," Brandy muttered as she hung up the phone. "The man is definitely in need of help if he thinks he could ever write a romance," she continued under her breath. Her amber eyes raked the garish cover of the paperback novel she'd bought that morning.

"In fact, Mr. Ryan Sinclair is going to need a major overhaul if he wants to join the human race. The man's definitely Cro-Magnon."

THE DARK-HAIRED MAN swore under his breath as the phone buzzed with the annoying busy tone for the third time. Slamming down the receiver, he tapped an impatient beat on the surface of his desk, forcing himself to wait a span of no more than two minutes. Then, punching the buttons with far more force than necessary, he tried the call again.

"Maggie. What in the hell are you trying to do to me?" Aggravation caused Ryan Sinclair to dispense with pleasantries as the husky feminine voice answered the telephone.

"Ryan, what terrific timing. I was just talking with Brandy Raines. She's so excited to be working with you, darling."

"God, Maggie...you didn't promise anything?" The deep voice grated with absolute alarm.

"Of course not. But you should hear her go on about your book, Ryan. She honestly swore to me she's never read anything like it."

"And never written anything like it, either. I just managed to wade my way through that schmaltzy romance you sent over. I can't believe the woman earns a living writing that stuff: 'The gentle sea breezes whispered a silken promise that was echoed in the gleaming dark eyes of Adam Black. The rakish privateer had sworn he would have her, with or without her permission, but as his lips lowered to hers, Megan could not think of a single valid protest....' Maggie!"

It was a roar, but it equaled in frustration and intensity the earlier wail by Brandy. Maggie O'Neal took a deep breath, lit a long dark cigarette and tried again.

"Ryan, Brandy's books are loved by millions of her readers. She touches a chord in their hearts with her love stories."

"Anybody who'd respond to that isn't touched in the heart—just the head," he muttered, his green eyes taking in the cover art of a young heroine being quite expertly ravished by a bold, swashbuckling pirate.

"You can't possibly expect me to find one common ground on which to attempt a collaboration. I'd rather try to work with a baboon holding a fistful of crayons."

"All I'm asking is that you meet with her, Ryan. She's a very nice woman, and I think you two will hit it off."

Ryan conjured up a mental image of Brandy Raines, swathed in yards of pink chiffon, lounging against satin pillows, a fluffy, dyed-to-match French poodle on her lap. Only a frustrated spinster could write such idealized love scenes as the ones he'd read in *Love's Savage Embrace*.

"Maggie," he said on a note of caution, "you didn't promise anything, did you? I mean, I don't want to hurt the old girl's feelings, but I really don't think we're going to be able to work out any type of partnership."

"I didn't promise a thing. Although, Ryan, while Brandy sells very well, I really would like to expand her market. If you help her add some action to her romances, darling, it could work out quite profitably for both of you."

Maggie O'Neal had been Ryan Sinclair's agent long enough to know the man responded favorably to the idea of increased income. She had decided early in their relationship that his enjoyment of spending money stemmed from all those years he'd struggled on a policeman's salary.

Yet he was far more likely to lavish gifts on others than he was to spend his royalties on himself. With the exception of that marvelous house, his car and newly acquired sailboat, Ryan lived less flamboyantly than most men in his income bracket.

"I'll see her," Ryan agreed reluctantly. "But only because you got me that nice fat TV deal for *The Killing Hour*. If you weren't such a terrific agent, I'd throw myself off the top of the Cabrillo lighthouse before I'd spend ten minutes with the woman."

"You're a dear," Maggie enthused on a pleased trill, stabbing out the cigarette with satisfaction. She leaned back in the soft suede chair, smiling across the room at the wall adorned with framed covers from both Ryan's and Brandy's latest best-sellers. Her expression was that of a master alchemist who'd just succeeded in turning lead to gold.

"Someday, Ryan," she predicted, "you'll thank me for this."

"Sure," he muttered, hanging up the phone. Ryan jammed his hands into the back pockets of his jeans as he stood at the picture window, watching the surf pound against the rugged, sea-sculpted shoreline of La Jolla.

If there was one thing Ryan Sinclair knew with an ironclad certainty, it was that he'd never be able to work with Brandy Raines. While he was nothing like his alter ego, Johnny Steele, there was one trait both men had in common. They preferred their woman strong and free spirited. It was obvious Brandy had as much spunk as a marshmallow.

THE GOLD PORSCHE stood out like a sore thumb on her quiet tree-lined street. Late as she was, Brandy couldn't help slowing her jog to study the low-slung car. She was bending to peer into the tinted window on the sidewalk side when the driver's door opened. Lifting a startled gaze, she locked eyes with a pair of bright green ones over the metallic top.

"Do you know you're the first person to show up on this street in over an hour?"

The man's eyes issued a welcome as they moved across her face with obvious interest. Those eyes smiled often, Brandy decided, noting the tracery of lines fanning up and outward. And while attractive, they were also full of an intelligence she found appealing.

She brushed back the strands of hair that had escaped from her ponytail during the racket-ball game, feeling untidy in comparison to the casual good looks of the newcomer. She was uncomfortably aware of the dampness between her breasts, darkening the pale yellow material of her T-shirt, and as she glanced down, she saw the scrape on her left knee was beginning to ooze unattractively.

The man whose unthreatening gaze was making a leisurely study of her slender form was as immaculate as Brandy was disheveled. His dark hair, obviously cut to allow minimum maintenance, ruffled in the breeze, the wind only serving to highlight brilliant gold strands. His teak complexion and slightly reddened nose exhibited a lifetime spent outdoors in the California sun.

Casually dressed, he wore a royal blue polo shirt with the obligatory status alligator on it, but as a note of whimsy, this reptile was on its back, legs up in the air. His well-fitting jeans were creased in a straight line down to running shoes, the swoosh a deep shade of blue.

Brandy's gaze returned to his friendly, smiling face. "Julian has less than two hundred citizens," she advised him. "We don't get a lot of traffic in the middle of the afternoon. Most people are working."

He rested his arms on the top of the car, leaning toward her in an interested gesture. "And how about you? Are you a lady of leisure?"

Brandy didn't miss the quick glance to her left hand, which was bare of any jewelry. Including the wedding ring this stranger was so obviously looking for.

"No, I work at home," she answered. "My time is my own. So to speak."

"I see." The casual tone indicated he didn't really see at all, but was disinclined to pursue it. "Where's home?"

Brandy pointed with her racket. "Right here. You're parked in front of it, as a matter of fact. When I first saw your car, I thought you might be someone I was supposed to meet this afternoon, but..."

She shrugged slim shoulders, smiling at the ridiculous comparison between this attractive, friendly man and the boozing, uncouth Ryan Sinclair.

His eyes widened and took on the sheen of emeralds. "Do you by any chance work for the old biddy who owns this place? Tell me you're her secretary and I'll know my luck has changed."

Brandy's brow wrinkled. "Old biddy? I'm afraid I don't—"

"Miss Brandy Raines," he said, spitting out her name as if it held a bad aftertaste. "I'm here to meet her and I was just thinking if you were going to be around afterward, perhaps we could have dinner. Or something."

His smile was definitely suggestive, and Brandy heard the bell chime as she placed him. The appearance might not resemble what she'd conjured up for Ryan Sinclair, but the behavior was definitely Johnny Steele. Right down to the friendly, self-assured leer.

"Why don't you come in," she offered smoothly, granting him a sweet, enticing smile. "I'll see if the old biddy's ready to see you."

"I don't think she's home. I arrived almost an hour ago, right on time. I spent a while leaning on the doorbell, but no soap."

"She's probably taking her afternoon nap," Brandy replied, turning away to keep him from seeing her lips twitch. "The dear old girl's rather deaf. I'll wake her for you; I'm certain she'll be delighted to have company. She doesn't get out much these days, what with her rheumatism and all."

She glanced over her shoulder, her tawny eyes as soft and innocent as a child's. "What did you say your name was?"

"Sinclair," he answered, closing the car door with a swift, decisive gesture and joining her as she walked up the shaded walk to the door. "Ryan Sinclair."

"Sinclair," Brandy murmured, as if to herself, swinging her racket loosely in her hand. "No, I'm afraid the name doesn't ring a bell. Miss Raines must have forgotten to tell me you'd be dropping by this afternoon.... Are you the man from the gas company? They've been promising to send someone out to check the meter; you can't believe the bills we've been getting."

"No. I'm a writer."

"A writer? Really?" Brandy's eyes widened to huge saucers. "Why, what a coincidence. So is Miss Raines." She stopped in her tracks for a moment, turning to gaze at him. "But perhaps you already knew that?"

"I knew it. If you can call that trash writing. Maggie O'Neal sent me here to see if I could pull the old crackpot's fat out of the fire for her. But I doubt it's possible. I'm just putting in the time because Maggie's been one helluva good agent for me."

Ryan's eyes gleamed bright with insinuation as he treated her to yet another male appraisal. "Although you make the trek up to these mountains delightfully worthwhile."

Brandy turned, and in doing so slammed her racket directly into his denim-clad knee, feeling a definite surge of satisfaction as she heard the hard crack.

"Ouch!" Ryan stopped, bending to grasp his injured leg with both hands, rubbing vigorously against the thick material.

"Oh, my goodness, how careless of me. I *do* hope I haven't hurt you."

Brandy's voice dripped honey and Ryan shook his head, standing up again. He tested the weight on the leg gingerly.

"Don't worry about it. It was my fault. I walked into your racket." He favored her with a wide smile that only wobbled slightly when he put his full weight down onto his left foot.

"I'm so relieved. You've no idea how I'd feel if I'd hurt you." Brandy glanced down at her leather-banded watch. "You must let me fix you lunch. Miss Raines serves the cutest little watercress sandwiches. Cut into little triangles and spread with just the lightest smidgen of margarine. She used to use butter, but of course at her age, the doctor's put her on a fat-restricted diet.... I'm certain we can round up some butter for you, though, Mr. Sinclair."

"Ryan," he corrected, forcing himself to walk without a limp as the pain radiated in all directions from the wounded knee.

Nine years spent on the San Diego police force had brought assorted occupational injuries, but it had been a long time since anything had hurt enough to set his teeth on edge like this. He could only hope she hadn't shattered the knee that had already seen too many operating tables in his thirty-three years. For such a slender woman, she had one helluva backhand. He wondered what damage she could have inflicted if she'd meant that wild swing of the racket.

He forced his attention back to their conversation. "Thanks anyway, but I can live without watercress sandwiches. It'll help me work up an appetite for dinner."

Eyeing the trouble he was going to so as to appear as macho as one of his sleezy heroes, Brandy decided that Ryan Sinclair's appetites were definitely of another order. And she'd bet her last advance check that she was listed on the menu as dessert.

"Watch that third step," she advised. "It's in need of repair."

Like a million other things around this tiny, turn-of-the-century house, she could have added. Because she had grown up in an ever-changing series of foster homes, this was the first place Brandy had been able to call her own. Although she adored it, the constant upkeep often had her feeling she was fighting a losing battle. This time, however, she would have loved to see Ryan Sinclair crash through the rotting boards, right up to his tanned neck.

Brandy opened the front door, determined to get this over with as soon as possible. She didn't want him hanging around any longer than was absolutely necessary, but the man had a lesson to learn about women in general and Brandy Raines in particular. It would be worth putting up with his annoying attitude long enough to watch him crawl away, tail between his legs.

"No lock?"

"I assure you, Miss Raines is up to any challenge. Besides, we don't lock our doors here in Julian. We all know and trust one another." She gestured for him to follow her in.

Ryan expelled a soft whistle as he entered, his roving eyes taking in the shimmering lemon-yellow walls in a room that was decorated predominantly with white, lemon and melon. While the furnishings ranged from traditional to antique, the mood was cheery and uplifting. *Quite some layout for an old gal*, he thought, an odd suspicion nagging away in the back of his mind. In his years on the force, Ryan had learned to make snap decisions about people; several times his life had depended on that ability. Something was wrong here, but he couldn't quite put his finger on it.

"This is really nice," he said aloud. "Not at all what I was expecting."

"I suppose that was lacy hand-crocheted antimacassars draped over all the furniture and skirted tables cluttered with a variety of Victorian memorabilia?"

Ryan shrugged his wide shoulders. "Something like that. Or flocked velvet wallpaper and red satin love seats. Something to match her flowery writing style."

"I see."

Brandy bit the words off, withholding the temptation to let the man know exactly what she thought of him. The time wasn't right. Not yet.

"Well, if you'll just have a seat, I'll wake Miss Raines and give her an afternoon tonic. We certainly want her on her toes if she's going to be writing with you."

"You're mistaken. She's not going to be writing with me. Like I said, this is just a courtesy call. I've my reputation to think of. And collaborating with Brandy Raines would sink it faster than an Excocet missile."

"I understand." Brandy reined in the tremendous urge she had to break her racket over Ryan Sinclair's smug, sun-gilded head. "I'll be back in just a few minutes," she said, leaving the room before she allowed herself the pleasure.

"Biddy!" she muttered, yanking on the water in the shower with undue force. "Pull the crackpot's fat out of the fire, will he? We'll just see whose fat gets burned before the day is over," she vowed, quickly undressing and stepping into the hot spray.

She massaged the thick shampoo into her hair, her fingers rubbing briskly against her scalp. Her seething anger intensified her motions.

"How dare he even begin to criticize what I do when all he can write about is that sex maniac Johnny Steele tripping over all those gory bodies!"

She was in and out of the shower in minutes, wrapping a towel about herself as she leaned over and began to blow dry her hair. Her brush moved with furious, harsh strokes. The more Brandy thought about Ryan Sinclair, the more her temper sizzled. What she wanted to do, with a very primitive fury, was to march back into that room and start throwing things at him.

But she refrained from that instinctive behavior, knowing it was all going to be worthwhile when she got to view the embarrassment in those brilliant emerald eyes. They were gorgeous eyes, she admitted reluctantly, remembering the flecks of gold that veined them like a vibrant sunburst and that lush fringe of curly sable lashes. His nose was a little pug, which, combined with that wide crescent of white smile, made him appear boyishly attractive.

"Probably all caps," she muttered, recalling the dazzle of his smile. Her resolve flickered for an instant, threatening to weaken. This was ridiculous. She had work to do. Once she had her well-earned laugh, she'd send the man packing. Metallic gold Porsche and all.

That wide smile greeted her as she reentered the room.

"Caps," Brandy said under her breath. "Definitely caps."

"Pardon me?" Ryan asked as he stood up.

While Brandy was distracted by the polite gesture, even Ryan wasn't certain whether it was born of a well-honed sense of professional etiquette or the shattering fact that the young woman before him was stunning. She'd obviously showered and changed, the casual clothes perfect for her slim, almost athletic frame. Her hair was still damp, although it appeared she'd spent some time with the dryer. Wispy blond strands framed her face, the curls possessing the same warm color as the honey one could buy from roadside stands. So intent was Ryan on his prolonged, thoughtful appraisal that he missed her answer to his question and had to ask it again.

"It was nothing important—I was just making a brief mental note for characterization," she replied briskly. "Are you thirsty? I can offer you wine, beer, cola, coffee...?"

"Boy, a beer would be great if you have one." Brandy forced herself to ignore the sunny lights in his eyes as they thanked her. "I didn't realize it'd be so warm up here."

She reached into a compact refrigerator built into a cabinet next to her desk, extracting a dark brown bottle. Twisting the cap, she handed it to him, waiting until he took a long, deep swallow.

"We have warm days and cool nights," she answered. "I'm sorry you had to wait so long. My game went on far longer than I'd expected. It seemed we spent the last hour just breaking each other's serves."

Brandy leaned back against the desk, crossing her long legs in front of her, easily garnering his attention with the expanse of smooth tanned skin showcased by brief white shorts.

"But I'm ready for you to begin pulling my fat out of the fire, Mr. Sinclair."

Brandy had to bite her bottom lip to keep from breaking into a purely victorious laugh as she watched his throat contract and convulse. As Ryan nearly choked on the icy liquid, her golden eyes laughed boldly at his discomfort.

"Miss Raines, I presume," he managed finally. His voice was hoarse, but Brandy had to give the man credit for composure.

"The same." She smiled. "And now that we've had our obligatory getting-to-know-you chat, you can report back to Maggie that we were incompatible, after all." She turned to leave the room, stopping at the doorway to eye him over her shoulder. "Oh, you can take the beer with you, Mr. Sinclair. I wouldn't want to keep you here a moment longer than necessary."

Ryan was by her side in two swift strides, long fingers curving about her wrist. "Not so fast. I've spent an hour sweltering outside this house, waiting for Brandy Raines to show up. You promised me a meeting, lady, and by God, you're going to give it to me."

"We've got nothing to discuss, Mr. Sinclair," Brandy replied archly, her eyes turning to agates as they moved to his fingers, demanding that he release her.

"We've got a lot to discuss. But not here." His other hand moved to her back as he quite effectively began moving her in the direction of the front door.

"Let go of me!"

Brandy shook free of the light palm resting at the small of her back, but his fingers still encircled her slim wrist, holding her effectively in his grasp.

"I think the expression is 'unhand me, you cad,'" he countered, not slackening his pace for a moment as Brandy dug her heels into a plush melon throw rug. The looped yarn rug gathered up as Ryan pulled her across the floor.

"The expression is, 'get your damned hands off me!'" she shouted, yanking at her hand without result.

He laughed heartily, unfazed by her protest. "It sounded trite when you put it in that book, Brandy, old girl, but damned if it isn't true."

Brandy reached out and grabbed a ladderback chair, attempting to hold her ground.

"What's true? And let go of me right now, Ryan Sinclair, before I call the police to come haul you away."

"It's true that you're cute as the dickens when you're riled up.... Oh, and you probably wouldn't get a lot of cooperation from the police. I'd just tell them we were having a lovers' spat. Cops don't like to enter into family fights unless they really have to."

"How would you know? Have many other women been forced to call for help when you go into your Johnny Steele impression?" She released her hold on the chair, using the fingers of her free hand to pry at the long dark fingers around her wrist.

"I worked that side of the badge for nine years," he replied casually. "So take my word for it, Brandy—right now the only way you're going to get rid of me is to grant me our promised meeting."

Brandy gave up on loosening his hold. She didn't know how he was doing it, since his fingers weren't digging into her flesh, but Ryan Sinclair was maintaining his grip on her wrist with the strength of metal handcuffs. He wasn't hurting her in the least. But he was making her mad as hell.

"I refuse to talk to a man who uses force on a woman," she shot back.

For a moment, the devils dancing in Ryan's green eyes were banished, replaced by a fleeting shadow. Her words compelled him to view his actions in another, more unattractive light. He'd seen too many instances of men who used their superior strength to control women. He didn't even want to count the number of times he'd been called back to the same house, over and over again, the results all too often the same. Nothing would be solved and he'd leave with a knot in the pit of his stomach, hoping this wouldn't be the time the violence would get out of hand.

He hated her even thinking he had anything in common with those animals, yet, damn it, this was her fault. She'd purposefully kept him waiting; he was already late to Kevin's party, and he wasn't about to deprive his seven-year-old nephew of a father figure just so he could argue all afternoon with this woman.

Although unsure of his motives, Ryan knew he wanted to get to know Brandy Raines better. And the only way he could do that right now was to take her down to Chula Vista with him.

"I'm not going to hurt you, Brandy. Believe me, all I want is the opportunity to talk that I've been promised."

For a moment, studying his sincere expression, Brandy found herself wanting to believe him. Then she realized that they could talk right here. There was no reason for him to be hauling her across the floor like a disobedient German shepherd. Ryan Sinclair was not a particularly tall man. Brandy doubted if he topped five foot ten. But his body was hard as a rock and proved no contest for a five-foot-six-inch woman, even one who played racket ball or squash every day and considered herself in excellent condition.

"Is that all you want?" she challenged, knowing as she did so that she'd miscalculated badly. Thrown off guard momentarily by the fleeting vulnerability on Ryan Sinclair's face, she'd vacillated, inviting the reappearance of Johnny Steele.

His emerald eyes warmed, inviting her to give in. "Now that you mention it, a kiss would be a terrific idea. Has anyone ever told you that you've got an absolutely gorgeous mouth? It practically begs to be kissed."

"You do and you lose those teeth you paid so much for," Brandy threatened, tugging ineffectively to free her arm. She refused to admit that the light in those eyes, as they rested on her lips, had offered a moment's temptation.

As Ryan pulled her down her sidewalk to the Porsche, he moved graciously onto the grass to allow the passage of her neighbor, Mrs. Simpson. The elderly woman stared at him with wide-eyed interest.

"Good afternoon." Ryan nodded his dark head politely, treating the overtly curious woman to a friendly smile, his entire attitude belying the fact he was doing anything at all unusual. "Beautiful day, isn't it?"

The woman warmed instantly to the smooth male charm and brilliant smile. She gave a swift tug on the leash in her hand, stilling an aged scottie who was prepared to continue down the walk. Brandy noted with amazement that Mrs. Simpson, who certainly wasn't known for her gregarious behavior, appeared quite willing to remain there and chat with Ryan Sinclair all afternoon.

"Lovely day," she confirmed. "A perfect day for a walk."

"That's what Brandy and I thought." Ryan nodded, opening the car door. "And now that we've had our little walk, I think I'll take her for a ride."

"Lovely day for that, too," Mrs. Simpson agreed with a broad smile. "Have a good time." She waved before continuing on her walk.

"Do you know what's wrong with you?" Brandy grated through clenched teeth as Ryan reached in and pulled the seat belt across her T-shirt.

"Nope. I've never had a woman complain before. Usually I receive rave reviews." He smiled boldly as he climbed over her.

As his firm, hard body slid across her lap, Brandy experienced an alien shock to her senses. She jerked upward, the instinctive movement throwing Ryan forward, causing his forehead to hit the tinted windshield with a dull thud.

"Hey!" he exclaimed, rubbing at the reddening mark. "What is it about me that makes you feel the need to beat me up?"

"How about the fact that you've insulted my writing, hauled me bodily from my house, thrown me into this adolescently flamboyant car, then had the unmitigated gall to drag your body over the top of me? And that's just for openers," Brandy finished as she ran out of breath.

Never would she admit that while the injury to his knee had been intentional, that crack from the windshield was in response to the warmth his body had unnervingly stimulated.

"Would you have come willingly?"

"Of course not."

"I didn't think so," he murmured agreeably. "Sorry, honey, but if I had walked around, you would have probably gotten out of the car, forcing me to chase you down. Not that it wouldn't be a lot of fun—" his eyes danced with the notion as they moved down her body "—but I don't want to give that sweet old lady more than she can handle in one day."

Brandy stared at him. "The trouble with you is that you're a very sick man. You've got this weird idea that you're actually Johnny Steele. And that women are going to fall into a dead faint at your feet."

"Do you feel like falling at my feet?" he asked with interest as he dug deeply into a pocket for the car keys.

The motion brought Brandy's eyes to his hard thigh encased in the tight indigo denim and she fought the scarlet flags waving in her cheeks as she realized her interested scrutiny had been observed by Ryan. His eyes practically shouted out victory.

"I'll be sure to let you know when I get the vapors," she snapped, crossing her arms over her chest. "And you can bet every cent you ever make from those sleazy novels that I'm going to tell Maggie about all this. She'll drop you flat."

He laughed, a deep, enjoyable sound. "Old ten-percent Maggie? Nah, not just for a little thing like kidnapping. Besides, I've no intention of taking you across state lines. Now if I were to have my way with you, Brandy Raines, that'd probably be grounds for a severe lecture and a possible slap on the wrist. But I'm not into forcing women, so you can relax on that count."

"I see. Are you into white slavery? Or do you have to hold people hostage to get them to listen to your plot ideas?" Brandy's voice grew theatrically hysterical. "Oh, no! Don't tell me you're going to read me your latest pot-boiler. Torture me any way but that!"

"Not at all what I suspected," he acknowledged thoughtfully. "In fact, you're obviously bright enough that we might be able to straighten you out, after all."

He laughed, this time a bold, rakish laugh, and Brandy was disconcerted to find herself oddly drawn to the sound, despite her fury at the way he'd treated her.

So far she'd known the man less than twenty minutes and he'd insulted her writing, placed her in a compromising position with the town's busiest gossip, abducted her and laughed at her. If the car wasn't going so fast, she'd take her chances and jump out.

"I wouldn't," Ryan advised, sliding a glance toward her. "We're going too fast and you'd only get the other knee banged up. What did you do, anyway? That's a nasty-looking scrape."

He realized suddenly that ever since he'd entered her bright, sunlit room, he'd entirely forgotten his own knee. He flexed his foot on the floorboard experimentally. There was a slight grinding of tendons, but nothing he hadn't learned to live with.

"I went after a shot that was sliding off the wall," Brandy answered. "Not that it's any of your business."

"Did you win the point?"

"Of course."

Once again Brandy was treated to that knowing flash of white. "Good girl. A little klutzy perhaps; we'll have to work on your moves. But it still shows spunk, darlin'."

Brandy's amber eyes widened at the nerve of this man. What did she care whether or not he approved of her racket-ball techniques? And for that matter, how did he know whether she'd been klutzy or not? That had been a pretty hard shot. As for that drawled endearment, well, he could just keep that stuff for Johnny Steele. Because Ryan Sinclair was going to get nowhere in this belated attempt to turn on the charm.

She screwed up her face into a disapproving scowl and glared out the tinted window, unmoved for once by the quaint tranquillity of her small town as it lay nestled amid the apple and pear orchards, appearing more like the communities of Northern California's mother lode country than the brass, bustling San Diego County.

2

"I HOPE you like hamburgers."

Ryan's baritone voice broke the lingering silence as they headed south on the San Diego freeway. Brandy continued her icy gaze out the window, refusing to respond to his friendly tone.

"At times. With the right company."

She heaped an extra helping of scorn on her answer, letting him know right off the bat that she'd never consider this arrogant storm trooper an even occasional companion. When he failed to respond to her gibe, Brandy glanced at him.

"Why?" she inquired suspiciously.

Wide shoulders strained the seams of his blue polo shirt as they lifted and dropped in a careless shrug. "It's just that they're Kevin's favorite, so I assume that's what we'll be eating for lunch today."

Brandy's tawny eyes widened at his assumption that she'd have lunch with him. And who was Kevin, anyway? One of his henchmen, she decided.

"I didn't agree to lunch."

"Of course you did."

"I most certainly did not!"

Ryan's eyes, as they left the freeway to observe her, were home to dancing devils of amusement.

"Of course you did," he repeated with extreme patience. "When you invited me in for those cute little sandwiches. The watercress with just a smidgen of margarine?" he reminded her. "Can I help it if I'm not into rabbit food? You have to admit that a hamburger, grilled to perfection and piled high with pickles and onions, is far more appetizing."

"I never intended to—" Brandy clamped her jaws together, stopping the admission before it could escape entirely. But she hadn't fooled Ryan Sinclair for a moment.

Instead of appearing irritated by her silkily spun trap, he gave her that devastating smile. "I had a feeling you were pulling my leg, sweetheart, but at the time I couldn't figure out why." He reached out a tanned hand and ruffled her hair, which had sprung into wild, unruly waves. "You had no intention of feeding me lunch, did you?"

"Not one morsel," she agreed. Brandy crossed her arms over her chest. "And if you think I'm going to apologize, Ryan Sinclair, you've got another think coming. You were arrogant, presumptuous and downright rude about my writing. You deserved everything you got."

And more, she tacked on silently, her eyes hard as agates as she dared him to utter a single word in self-defense.

"You're absolutely right." Once again he gave her a grin whose brilliance rivaled the California sun for warmth.

Now what was he up to? For a man who'd stopped just short of physical violence to get her into his car, Ryan was certainly being agreeable all of a sudden. Brandy didn't trust him. Not for one second.

She stared for a short, intense moment at his quirked lips, reluctantly moving her gaze upward to green eyes that gleamed with good humor. Brandy decided that all those years writing about Johnny Steele had fried the man's brain. He was far too loosely wrapped for her to discern a single thing he had in mind.

However, since he didn't appear actually dangerous, and she did have a witness—Mrs. Simpson would never forget Ryan Sinclair—Brandy decided to relax and enjoy the admittedly pleasurable experience of riding in this sleek, fast car, the soft summer wind swirling her hair into frothy confusion.

She was surprised when Ryan pulled the car up in front of a neat, but unassuming house in the San Diego suburb of Chula Vista.

"What are we doing now?"

He pocketed the car keys. "Having lunch."

"I'm not hungry." Actually, after her vigorous racketball game, Brandy was starving. But something about this man brought out the worst in her.

"That's okay. We'll slide your burger onto my plate when no one's looking. You don't have to worry about embarrassing me with your picky appetite."

Ryan was out of the car, opening her door with a flourish before Brandy could muster up a strong enough protest.

"A very sick man," she muttered, thinking not for the first time that Ryan Sinclair was reminding her more and more of his alter ego.

From what she'd read in *The Uninvited Corpse*, Johnny Steele's principle character trait was that the man lacked the ability to hear a single word of denial. In this respect, both Johnny Steele and Ryan Sinclair were soul mates. They blissfully charged through life, secure in their misguided belief that they could do no wrong.

"You're being unfair," he protested lightly, his hand cupped under her elbow, the gentle upward pressure urging her out of the bucket seat.

Brandy shook her arm free. "*I'm* being unfair? You're the one who accused me of being a frustrated old biddy who only wrote romances because I couldn't catch a man. You're the one who arrived at my home today with a preconceived notion of Brandy Raines as some sex-starved virgin!"

She felt an odd tremor tingle up her spine as Ryan put a hand on top of her seat, effectively holding her to his silent scrutiny.

"I was wrong about that," he admitted easily, his voice ebony satin as it smoothed over her, working against the defenses she attempted to muster against his seductive look. "I just have one question."

"What makes you think I'll answer it?"

"I can only hope." Warm eyes held her mutinous gaze. "Tell me, Brandy Raines, is there presently a man in your life?"

"That's none of your business," she snapped.

"That's where you're wrong," he countered, unperturbed by her prickly behavior. "But I don't think there is. Not now, anyway."

Ryan leaned over her, his eyes moving over her uplifted face with the impact of a physical caress. Brandy drew in her breath, her every nerve suddenly standing on end. She caught a whiff of peppermint-scented breath, mingling with the spicy aroma of his after-shave. The fiery sun had turned the triangular expanse of skin at the neck of his shirt to a glistening teak. Brandy reminded herself that Ryan Sinclair had honed his skills well, as he'd undoubtedly worked overtime to research his detective novels. She refused to provide fodder for his next potboiler.

"I'm going home right now," she insisted. "You can either get back in this car and drive me yourself, or I'm calling a cab. But if you think I intend to spend one more minute in your company, Ryan Sinclair, you're a candidate for the booby hatch."

He shook his head with what appeared to be honest regret. "Brandy, Brandy...why don't you allow some of that romance you've got buried deep inside you out, so you can see the inevitability of our relationship?"

"You're stereotyping again, Ryan," she returned, not budging an inch. "I don't write from experience or personal need. I simply provide entertaining reading for women who are no more sex-starved than I am."

"I wasn't talking about sex."

Brandy knew she was in dangerous waters entering into any type of argument with this man, but she arched a honey brow, inviting him to elaborate. She did wish, however, that he wasn't standing over her. She was having to look into the sun and it blinded her view of his face.

As if possessing the uncanny ability to read her mind, Ryan squatted beside the car. He took both her hands in his, the short, negative shake of his head disallowing her planned protest.

"I'm talking about romance. You're two women, Brandy. You proved your strength by launching a rear attack that succeeded in making me look like a prize jackass. Something, by the way, I wouldn't permit just anyone to get away with. You've laughed at me, cussed at me and told me in every way possible that you consider me nothing but a sleazy male chauvinist.

"But deep down inside you, Brandy, is a warm, passionate woman who yearns for some of those pleasures you routinely bestow on your heroines. You're a beguiling combination: a modern, twentieth-century feminist and an old-fashioned lass looking for the hero of her dreams. You need a man capable of responding to both those aspects of your personality."

"And I suppose you're just that man," she said acidly, not even bothering to argue his assertion. It was too ridiculous for words.

"I plan on giving it one hell of an old college try," Ryan responded, his warm smile indicating that he had either missed her scorn or decided to ignore it, moving on with all the bulldozer methods of Johnny Steele.

"Do you know what I think?" she asked in turn.

"About what?"

"About you."

Ryan rocked back on his heels, eyeing her cautiously. His hands still held Brandy's, his long dark fingers lacing through hers with a gentle strength.

"You're going to tell me, whether I like it or not, aren't you?"

"Of course."

"Shoot," Ryan invited.

At his choice of words, Brandy grinned, considering that was exactly what she'd like to do to Ryan Sinclair. Shoot a silver bullet directly through his inflated male ego. Her unguarded smile was honest and open for the first time, and Brandy was unaware of how it softened her appearance. Ryan stared, momentarily stunned into a bemused silence.

"You're arrogant, chauvinistic and all too busy living vicariously through your hero—that Neanderthal macho man, Johnny Steele. Since you're obviously afraid to chance a sincere, meaningful relationship with a woman, you and Johnny storm through life, collecting notches on your headboard as proof of your masculinity."

"You really don't like Johnny, do you?"

To hell with being careful of the man's feelings, she decided. He wasn't playing fair—why should she?

"He's overbearing, arrogant, unbending and ruthless. He takes whatever he wants from a woman, blissfully believing that she'll succumb to his less than polished charms."

"You make him sound a great deal like Adam Black," Ryan observed, referring to the dashing pirate hero of *Love's Savage Embrace*.

Brandy was about to issue a scathing renunciation that any character of hers would even vaguely resemble one of Ryan's when the door to the house opened and a huge ball of fur came barreling down the sidewalk, flinging itself at Ryan. He released Brandy's hands as he fell back onto the sidewalk, laughing as his face was washed by a very long, very pink tongue belonging to what appeared to be an indescribable mass of whitish fluff.

The animal was followed in short order by another ball of energy, this one recognizable as a young boy as he, too, climbed aboard the man lying on the ground.

"Hey! Enough!" Ryan hollered from under the writhing mass of boy and dog.

"Kevin Michael Sinclair!" A slender, dark-haired woman joined the crowd, freeing Ryan from the enthusiastic welcome. "You let your uncle off the ground right now, or there'll be no dessert."

"Ah, mom, you can't do that. It's my birthday cake!" Wide brown eyes displayed incredulity at the very idea.

"I can do whatever I want, young man, and don't forget it. Now apologize to your Uncle Ryan, then take Bentley into the house and lock him up. Scoot." The woman's smile negated her strong tone and the child answered with a grin of his own.

"Bentley was just glad to see Uncle Ryan." He tugged on a collar hidden under the mass of fur as he dragged the dog along the sidewalk toward the house. Midway there, he stopped, his smooth young brow furrowed with concern. "Uncle Ryan?"

"Yeah, Kevin?"

"Did you bring me a present?"

Ryan's eyes opened wide. "Gee, was I supposed to?"

"Of course you were. It's my birthday."

Ryan laughed, a deep, happy sound. "Then I guess I did." He turned to wink briefly at Brandy. "You'll discover that I possess very good party manners."

Satisfied, Kevin continued to drag the large English sheepdog back toward the house.

"I *am* sorry, Ryan." Kevin's mother was busy picking long strands of gray, white and black fur from Ryan's blue shirt. "Bentley sheds so much in the summer I swear I'm either going to take him to the animal shelter or learn to knit the stuff into afghans." She gave up on the attempt, turning her attention to Brandy.

"Hi. I'm Ellen Sinclair, sister-in-law to this handsome rogue and mother of that whirling dervish you caught a glimpse of earlier."

"Hi, I'm Brandy Raines," Brandy offered with a smile, taking the outstretched hand that accompanied Ellen's friendly greeting.

"You're kidding! *The* Brandy Raines? *Love's Savage Embrace*? *Passion's Bride*? *Stormy Rapture*? That Brandy Raines?"

"You've read them?" Brandy experienced that rush of pride she always felt when someone professed familiarity with her work.

"Every one. I absolutely adore Rafe Morgan. Do you know I find myself actually looking for that man whenever we go up to the mountains? I have to keep reminding myself that he's only a fictional character and not a real person."

Ellen stopped her effusive monologue and narrowed her dark eyes. "He's not real, is he? I mean, you're not lucky enough to know someone like that gorgeous mountain man, are you?"

Brandy was amused to see Ryan watching her as closely as Ellen. Deciding not to admit the rugged outdoorsman sprang from nothing but a particularly vivid imagination, she laughed the question off.

"Now, Ellen, don't you ever read the disclaimer? 'All characters are fictitious. Any resemblance to actual persons, living or dead, is purely coincidental.'"

"That's about as depressing a news as I've heard all day," the woman groaned in good-natured complaint. A roar went up from the backyard. "Oh, no, the little devils are at it again! Hurry up, Ryan. If you don't get those hamburgers grilled pretty soon, we'll have a full-fledged mutiny on our hands. The coals were ready ages ago."

She took off on a run in the direction of the continuing cacophony emanating from the backyard of the stucco house.

"You're the chef?" Brandy asked incredulously.

Ryan grinned. "Don't go getting any ideas of romantic, candlelit dinners. Grilled hamburgers are the apex of my culinary skills."

"That's why you dragged me here, isn't it? You were already late because of my game."

"Which game was that?" he inquired easily. "That extended racket-ball game, or the one that made me look like a class-A jerk?"

"Both," she admitted. "Although you did deserve it."

"Granted, but I think what we have here, Brandy, is a case of the pot calling the kettle black. You were expecting a magnified version of Johnny Steele, weren't you? Some unshaven, hung-over individual who'd just crawled from a rumpled bed in a cheap motel room."

"Of course I wasn't," Brandy lied through her teeth.

Ryan didn't argue the point; they both knew there was no need. "Sure, whatever you say.... Now, is the lady hungry?"

"The lady's starving," Brandy said, the sudden growl from the pit of her stomach echoing her words. She exited the car to stand beside him on the sidewalk.

Ryan dug behind the seat for a moment to extract a pile of gaily wrapped presents. "Well, then, let's have a go at those burgers. I'd hate to have it said that I didn't rush to the aid of a lady in distress."

As they walked toward the sounds of high-pitched laughter, Brandy allowed his broad hand to rest lightly on her back, deciding to drop her antagonistic attitude for the time being. It wasn't because of any fear that her prickly behavior would hurt Ryan's feelings. The man appeared to have the hide of a rhinoceros. But she wasn't the type of woman who'd ruin a child's party because of her own prejudices.

For all her denial, she *had* typecast Ryan Sinclair as nothing but a real-life version of his detective hero. Yet despite the fact he was undeniably attractive, and his behavior was far smoother than Johnny Steele's, Brandy had the instinctive impression that Ryan was every bit as dangerous as his fictional counterpart. In their short time together he'd already stirred emotions she recognized as extremely hazardous to her health.

3

BRANDY WAS INTRODUCED to a seemingly endless line of relatives, most of whom seemed intrigued by her appearance at a Sinclair family gathering. She would have liked to have attributed their interest to the fact that Ryan did not usually bring a date to these functions, but practicality forced her to attribute it more to her moderate fame, as most of the woman present acknowledged familiarity with at least one of her novels. She had no doubt Ryan's family had witnessed a constant stream of women.

Oddly enough, it seemed perfectly natural to spend the day by Ryan's side, taking over the chore of toasting the buns and spreading condiments. Together they fed a virtual army.

The party naturally spread to the neighborhood park that jutted up to the backyard of Ellen Sinclair's home, and soon teams were being chosen for a game of touch football.

"I don't know if Brandy should play," Ryan answered for her as Kevin called out her name for his team. "She banged up her knee today."

Brandy refused to examine why Ryan's solicitous manner grated even more than his early imperiousness. She swiftly rose from her seat on the ground.

"I'd consider it an honor to play on the birthday boy's team," she stated firmly, her tawny gaze meeting Ryan's with a distinct challenge.

Silence settled about them as if the entire clan sensed the gauntlet being thrown down. Finally a young man Brandy recognized as being a distant cousin obediently called out Ryan's name to be on his opposing team.

Brandy felt a surge of exhilaration as she faced Ryan across the line, her competitive nature steamrollering over that earlier sensual yearning.

"I don't suppose this is the time to tell you I played college ball at USC?" he murmured, for her ears only.

"Did you?" She mentally gave herself points for managing to display little interest.

"I can take you home to show you my trophies," he suggested, a wicked grin curving his mouth to display those strong white teeth.

If they weren't caps, Brandy decided, life was horribly unfair. The retainer she wore, while at home alone, as the final step in straightening her teeth, was her most closely guarded secret.

"Are sports trophies the he-man equivalent of etchings?"

"Some women have been known to be marginally impressed." His eyes danced with sexual insinuation.

Brandy shrugged. "Some women are easily impressed, I suppose."

"Hey, are you guys gonna play or what?" The third cousin stood behind the line, hands on his hips, looking irritated at the way Brandy and Ryan were holding up play.

"We'll play for now," Ryan called out apologetically. "And take care of the 'or what' later this evening," he murmured under his breath to Brandy. He winked and before she could come up with a suitable retort the foot-ball had been hiked between Ellen Sinclair's legs, and the opposing team's quarterback was going for a pass.

Whether it was her urge to get as far away from Ryan Sinclair as possible or an unconscious reading of the play, Brandy suddenly found herself running in a direct path with the spiraling football. All alone, she put on a burst of speed, intercepting the pass before turning up the field, the ball tucked under her arm.

Brandy enjoyed sports, having been introduced to them in the one foster home she'd not been made to feel an interloper. A high-school coach and math teacher, Craig Henderson had taken the eleven-year-old girl under his wing. They'd both discovered Brandy had a competitive streak that bordered on fanaticism and an inborn athletic sense that had caused her to wonder, in more introspective moments, whether either of her parents had been an athlete.

Her adrenaline surged as she deftly dodged the less experienced players on the field. Her lungs burned and her sore knee throbbed, but a few more yards and she'd have a touchdown. Suddenly a huge weight flung itself at her back and Brandy went sprawling, losing her hold on the football. All the breath was sucked from her lungs as she lay on her back, gasping like a grounded trout.

"Sorry about that," Ryan apologized.

Brandy's eyes were huge amber circles as she fought for her breath.

"Sorry?" she croaked.

He nodded. "I got carried away." His fingers probed across her rib cage. "Are you all right?"

One thing the coach had taught her was good sports-manship. "I'm fine. I just got the wind knocked out of me...."

Then, as she stared up at him, her irritation got the better of her. "What in the hell do you think you're doing? This was supposed to be flag ball."

"I told you, I got carried away. I saw you headed for the goal line and tackled instinctively."

"Hey, is Brandy all right?" This from the intercepted quarterback.

"Ryan Sinclair, you should be ashamed of yourself." Ellen was standing over them, her hands on her hips.

"I am," he acknowledged, to the surprise of both women.

"Really?" Ellen asked, the disbelief in her tone echoed by that in Brandy's topaz eyes.

"Of course. I've never thrown myself at a woman before." He grinned boyishly. "Usually it's the other way around."

That did it. Brandy pushed against his chest. "Get up, you big moose."

To his credit, Ryan tried, but his leg buckled under him and he almost crushed Brandy as he folded back down to the turf.

"Sorry," he mumbled, as she rolled out of danger.

"Oh, dear, is it your knee?" Ellen knelt beside him, her palm pressing against the denim.

"I'm getting too old for this stuff." He grimaced as his sister-in-law obviously hit a sore spot.

"Thirty-three is not old, Ryan." Ellen's dark eyes filled with concern. "Shall we take you to the sports-medicine center?"

He shook his head, pulling himself up on his elbows. His gaze, as it raked his leg, was irritated but resigned.

"No. But I think I'd better redshirt the rest of the afternoon and let Brandy administer some tender loving care."

"What makes you think I'll drop out of the game to sit around with the likes of you?" Brandy asked.

"Won't you?"

She tried to muster some anger at Ryan's masculine self-assurance, but his complexion had turned an oddly ashen shade, and she found herself honestly concerned. Johnny Steele didn't put himself out of commission like this. And he'd certainly never admit he was physically incapable of anything. She allowed Ryan to lean on her as they made their way to a stand of oak trees.

"Did you acquire that knee along with those trophies at USC?"

"Yeah, I sure did. It kept me out of the pros."

"Did that bother you?"

Ryan was sprawled on the grass, his face directed upward to the warm sun. Brandy sat beside him, her legs tucked under her.

"For a time. But I got over it."

"So you became a policeman instead."

"That's about it," he agreed, his gaze still directed upward.

"Was the injury why you quit the force?"

"No." Ryan's answer was short and had a tone Brandy couldn't recognize.

She chose not to follow that particular line of questioning and fell quiet, watching the raucous group continue their game. For someone who'd grown up without any family to call her own, the Sinclair clan was a mind-boggling group.

"How many sisters do you have?" she inquired, attempting to place them all in the blur of faces she'd been introduced to today.

"Seven," he answered casually, as if the idea of such a large family was not at all unusual.

"Seven?" Brandy stared at him, then swung her astonished gaze over to the tiny woman who'd been introduced as Ryan's mother. How in the world had she managed it?

"Seven," he confirmed, counting them off on long, dark fingers. "Let's see—there's Alice, Sarah, Annie, Julie, Elizabeth, Laurie and. . ." His smooth brow furrowed in thoughtful lines. Ryan stared at the upheld finger, as if it would hold some clue. "Aha—Jennifer."

He shook his head, slanting a grin toward her. "Lord, don't ever tell Jenny I forgot her, will you? She's a tiny enough little thing, but she's got a temper that could blow us all off the face of the earth."

"I promise," Brandy said absently, her mind on yet another problem. Then her wandering gaze settled on Ellen Sinclair. "I thought Ellen was your sister-in-law. But if you don't have any brothers—"

"Mike died," he replied brusquely.

"I'm sorry." An ineffectual thing to say, but it was all Brandy could think of. Since they'd first arrived at this family gathering hours ago, the mood had been light and carefree. She had been ill prepared for a statement of that magnitude.

"So am I. He'd be damned proud of how well Kevin's turning out, I think. Ellen's doing one helluva job."

"Has he been. . .uh, did it happen long ago?"

His attention was directed skyward once again, and Brandy was free to surreptitiously watch the hardening muscles jerk along his jawline.

"A little over three years. Mike was a cop, too. He'd stopped for a pack of cigarettes on his way home and was still in uniform. The sight of those blues scared a sixteen-year-old doper who was holding up the convenience market. Mike had a shotgun hole in his chest before he knew what hit him."

Ryan shook his head, his mouth a grim, taut line. "I always told Mike those cigarettes he chain-smoked would kill him."

Brandy took no offense at Ryan's harsh laugh, realizing his remark was professional gallows humor.

"I see why you quit," she murmured.

Ryan's green eyes widened incredulously as he turned his head toward her. "That's not why I quit the force. Hell, Mike knew the odds every time he put on that uniform. He knew, and Ellen knew. The same way my wife did."

She had to ask. "You have a wife?" Why did she dread the answer to that question?

"Had."

"Oh."

Had Mrs. Ryan Sinclair found herself unable to live with the strain of never knowing if her husband would return alive from his work? Had she divorced him? Or had he left her, unable to live under the constraints of marital monogamy?

"About six months after Mike's death, I was called to the scene of an accident," he volunteered. "I was the first patrol car to arrive."

An icy premonition spiraled up her spine, and Brandy covered Ryan's hand with her own.

"You don't have to tell me this."

He ignored her softly spoken protest, turning their hands so their fingers linked together.

"It was late on a Friday afternoon, and Suzanne's compact was broadsided by a guy who'd begun celebrating the weekend early."

Ryan closed his eyes to the bright expanse of blue sky, but Brandy knew that the images were vivid behind the lids.

"The car was a virtual accordion. I couldn't get her out; it took the fire department what seemed like hours to cut her body out of that crumpled mass of metal."

Brandy shut her own eyes momentarily, unable to bear the pain she saw etched on that darkly handsome face.

"The other driver was slumped over the wheel of the truck," he continued flatly. "At first I thought he was hurt, but when I pulled him out of the cab, I could smell the booze. I don't remember when they pulled me off him... Before I killed the bastard, I do know that....

"I turned in my badge the next day, then went home and proceeded to attempt suicide in my own inimitable fashion for the next month."

When Brandy couldn't answer, Ryan volunteered the information. "Nothing as drastic as what that overly active imagination of yours is probably conjuring up. I tried to drown myself in a constant diet of horribly inferior Scotch. In those days, it was all I could afford."

"And these days?"

His fingers squeezed hers lightly. "These days, although I can afford far better, I don't put it to such self-destructive use. A month after the funeral, I got a call from the eighteenth publisher I'd sent *The Killing Hour* to. They'd read it, loved it and were willing to pay good money for it. I thought about how many times Suzanne had encouraged me to keep working on that book even when it seemed an impossible dream. I couldn't let her down.

"I sobered up in time for the rewrites, and from then on, day by day I felt less like I was sinking into quicksand. This past year, I can honestly say, I've gotten over the entire horrible experience."

Brandy's eyes opened, clashing with Ryan's gaze like a pair of brass cymbals. She could only stare into the brilliantly lustrous eyes.

"Why are you telling me this?" she whispered, feeling it was not a story he related often. And certainly not to a stranger.

Ryan shrugged, his expression thoughtful. "I don't know. Perhaps so you'll understand that I'm not the hedonistic male stereotype you've obviously gleaned from my Johnny Steele series... Perhaps so you'll feel obligated to share something intensely personal with me, putting us on more even and intimate footing."

His eyes gleamed with unnerving warmth. "Or perhaps so you'll realize I'm going to kiss you simply because I find you an extremely desirable woman. And not becuase I'm looking to fill a void in my life."

At that moment, Brandy couldn't have cared less why she was going to receive the kiss she'd been secretly expecting since midway through their marathon cooking session. There'd been those unexpected times when their eyes met and held a moment too long over the barbecue. The message had sparked between them, as vivid as bolts of lightening in a blackened sky.

"Hey, Uncle Ryan, can you help me get my kite up?"

Both Ryan's and Brandy's heads jerked back quickly at the intrusion of the high-pitched, juvenile voice.

"Go ask your grandfather," Ryan instructed, his eyes not moving from Brandy's slightly parted lips.

"I did. Grandpa sent me to find you. He said you bought it, so you had to help me fly it." The complaining voice held the slightest tinge of whine.

"Oh, hell," Ryan groaned. "Dad knows I'm the worst possible candidate for the job." He reluctantly dragged his gaze up to Brandy's eyes. "How are you at flying a kite?"

"Okay, I guess. I'm not in the expert class, but I can get them up."

Ryan stood up, kite in hand. "Terrific. If I give in to the birthday kid, think you can help us fly it?"

Brandy leaned back on one elbow, shading her eyes with her hand as she looked up into his face. "Can't you fly a simple little kite?"

"There is *no* such thing as a simple little kite," Ryan grumbled. "The entire business is for masochists. I've fed more kites to ravenous trees and power lines than Charlie Brown, and those are only the ones I've managed to get airborne." His handsome face was set in a self-deprecating scowl that had Brandy laughing.

"Give me the kite, Kevin," she suggested, "and I'll show you how it's done."

The smile wreathing the freckled face was reward enough for giving up what she knew would have been a mutually enjoyable kiss. But Brandy had shared kisses with men before. The one thing she'd never shared was a birthday party such as this. Growing up in the revolving door of the California foster care system had not en couraged such activities. She wondered if Kevin knew how fortunate he was to have such a loving family. If only. . . Brandy shook her head, refusing to succumb to self-pity on such a lovely day.

"The first thing you do," she said firmly, "is get rid of this thing." She took the plastic reel and tossed it into a box of discarded gift wrapping.

"Hey! That cost me eighty-nine cents," Ryan complained.

"Too bad. You just wasted eighty-nine cents," Brandy answered flippantly. She smiled at the youngster who was watching her every move. "You see, Kevin, you have to hold the string in your hand. This way you'll feel as if you're right up there with the kite."

Kevin looked dubiously over at Ryan, who only shrugged his wide shoulders helplessly. They both watched as Brandy attached the string.

"This is a good kite. A dragon kite is perfect to learn with because it's all tail." She smiled encouragingly at the attentive boy.

Then she stood up, holding the long, cylindrical kite striped in brilliant primary colors.

Ryan looked around. "You don't have much room to run here, Brandy. Maybe we should go over there." He pointed to a large, open space.

"That's another mistake amateurs make," she replied, grinning saucily at him. "They run around and around, dragging their kite along the ground like a puppy chasing his tail."

She tugged lightly, letting out the string as the kite obediently rose into the cloudless blue sky. Like a rainbow-colored bird, it floated and bobbed, rising higher and higher until it hovered proudly overhead.

"Here you go, Kevin," she said, handing the string over to the grinning boy. "Just remember, don't let the kite fly you. If you really put yourself up there with the kite, really feel the flight, it'll behave for you."

"Gee, thanks, Brandy," he yelled, heading off across the grass, the kite gliding obediently through the air. Kevin stopped, looking back over his shoulder. "Are you coming, Uncle Ryan?"

Ryan looked regretfully at Brandy, who waved him away with a light laugh. "Go and learn," she said. "I might not be around the next time."

Ryan tested the weight on his leg, and then taking his nephew's hand in his larger one, they went off across the park. Only a slight limp indicated he might be in pain. Brandy watched them for a while, then lay back on the grass, enjoying the warm sunshine on her face. She didn't know how long it had been since she'd taken an entire day off work, but she was finding it to be a thoroughly enjoyable experience.

Even Ryan, she had to admit, added a certain extra zest. When he wasn't coming across like a storm trooper, he was actually quite nice. Almost sweet, she considered, remembering his tender way with Kevin. But he wasn't for her. The main lesson life had taught Brandy Raines was that personal involvement only led to heartache.

She dozed for a while, oblivious to the noisy crew still playing their football game. Sometime later she sat up and reached for the juicy peach she'd saved from lunch. Looking up, she felt a burst of pleasure as she viewed Ryan standing over her, kite in hand.

"Where's your sidekick?" she asked with a welcoming smile.

He lowered himself to the ground, stretching out beside her on the sun-warmed, fragrant grass. "Kid wore me out," he groaned, lacing his fingers beneath his head as he gazed up into the wide expanse of sky. "Fortunately I spotted a group of munchkins who were playing a game of hide and seek. I sent him off to cultivate new friendships."

"That's always a nice thing."

He rolled onto his side, propping his head up with his hand. "I'm glad you agree."

His gaze softened with that warm glow and Brandy lowered her eyes, biting into the peach. She was not inexperienced, but the odd flashes of desire that sparked through her at these moments were unknown to her. She had always remained cautious in her relationships, not opening up to people easily. Only in her writing were her emotions given free rein.

Ryan's eyes were focused on her mouth, making her horribly self-conscious, and she knew he could see the rippling of her throat muscles as she swallowed the sweet fruit.

"You've got peach juice around your mouth." His finger reached out to trace her lips, gathering a bit of nectar, then touching his fingertip to his own tongue experimentally.

"Sweet," he murmured. "Sweet and fragrant. But how much is the peach, I wonder, and how much is the lady?"

Brandy closed her eyes, knowing that at any moment Ryan's lips would be on hers, and he didn't disappoint her. His warm tongue circled the tingling flesh of her lips, claiming the nectar of the sweet fruit as his own. She moved her head under his light, delicate conquest, reveling in the feeling. Never had such a gentle kiss caused such a surge of emotions. Stars exploded behind her closed lids, shattering with a crystalline brilliance.

"Is she your girlfriend?" They both looked up instantly to see Kevin observing them.

"You'll have to ask the lady that question," Ryan answered, his eyes sparkling as he grinned down at her.

"Well, are you?" Dark eyes, vivid replicas of his mother's moved to Brandy's flushed face, observing her keenly.

"Aren't you going to answer?" Ryan asked provocatively as she hesitated.

"I'm not your uncle's new girlfriend," she replied, her tawny eyes shooting furious daggers at Ryan's teasing expression. He was absolutely no help. In fact, he seemed to be delighting in her discomfort.

"Darn," Kevin muttered, "I hoped you were. We really need someone to help us fly kites. He's terrible," he added, with a nod in Ryan's direction.

Kevin seemed oblivious to the sudden tension in the air as he joined them on the grass, watching Brandy intently. "You're nice," he commented finally. "And you're sure pretty enough. Prettier than any of the ladies Uncle Ryan usually goes out with."

"That's enough, sport," Ryan objected, amusement in his deep, rich voice. "I'm having enough trouble convincing Brandy I'm a nice guy without you putting your sticky little nose in it. Now go round up your mother so we can thank her for inviting us to this birthday bash."

Ellen Sinclair's friendly eyes seconded the words of her outspoken youngster a few minutes later. Then she proceeded to demonstrate exactly where Kevin had learned his forthright behavior.

"I want you to promise to bring Brandy over for dinner next week, Ryan," she instructed. "Because whether you know it or not, this time you've got yourself a real lady, and I want a chance to put in a good word for you before you blow it."

Ryan laughed. "I'll do my best, honey. But I'm working on a new book and you know how involved I get."

"A new book? Not another Johnny Steele?" Ellen groaned. "Just once I'd like to see that guy get involved with a woman he doesn't have to shoot before the story ends."

Brandy laughed. "My sentiments exactly," she put in, grinning wickedly at the disconcerted expression that moved like an earthquake across Ryan's face.

He put his hands up in a mock gesture of self-protection. "Hey, you two are ganging up on me," he complained, bending down to kiss Ellen lightly on the cheek. He turned away, his arm looped loosely about Brandy's shoulder.

"Oh, you don't have to worry," he said, grinning back at his sister-in-law. "This book is guaranteed to have a happy ending."

Ellen arched a disbelieving brow. "Really?"

"Really. I'm collaborating with Brandy, and I've got the gut feeling she'd never end a story without orange blossoms and a wedding march."

Increasing his pressure on her shoulder, Ryan urged Brandy down the sidewalk before her spluttering protests could be overheard by the incredulous woman watching them depart the Sinclair family celebration.

4

BRANDY WAS TOO FURIOUS to speak coherently until they were heading up into the Laguna Mountains, back to Julian.

"Why in the world did you tell Ellen we'd be working together?"

Ryan slowed the speed of the sports car to allow a doe and two fawns to scamper across the highway.

"I thought that was what today was all about," he answered finally.

"Today was about the two of us meeting. Then telling Maggie we decided collaboration was an impossibility," she corrected.

"Look," he stated, pointing upward. "Don't you love to see hawks circling? I could watch that for hours."

"Nice," she agreed absently, casting a quick glance upward at the widespread wings of the hawk. "Do you think we could return this conversation to our working together?"

"Of course." He gave her an encouraging smile. "Go right ahead. I'll attempt not to let Mother Nature interrupt, but if you're going to live out in this rustic setting, Brandy, you have to take into account the possibility that we city boys might get a bit distracted."

Brandy had the feeling that Ryan was only using the deer and the hawk to dodge the issue.

"I can't work with you."

"Can't? Or won't?"

She shrugged. "Can't, won't. What does it matter? The fact is that you and I are completely incompatible."

"You didn't feel that way earlier. I think we fed that crew with remarkable aplomb for two individuals who are supposed to be incompatible."

"Hamburgers. You're talking about grilling up a few patties of ground round. I'm talking about a joint creative effort. A book, Ryan."

He pulled the car up in front of her house. Killing the engine, he pocketed the keys, then turned to bestow a magnificent smile upon her. Reaching out, he brushed his knuckles along the uplifted line of her cheekbone.

"I don't know...I thought those were pretty creative hamburgers."

How in the world could he compare the two? "I take my work seriously, Ryan," she protested, doing her best not to be affected by his soft words or the caressing gesture that was sparking her skin with tongues of flame.

"So do I." His warm gaze held hers. "And I'm beginning to think what we did for burgers we can do for a suspense story, Brandy. How about giving it some thought?"

No way, a self-protective voice in a far corner of her mind called out. *You've been a loner for thirty years of your life, Brandy Raines; this is no time to be picking up any partners.*

"Well, I'll think about it," she heard herself say, knowing as she spoke that a joint effort between her and Ryan would fail before they'd gotten past the dedication page.

"We'll talk about it over dinner."

"We just finished an enormous lunch, Ryan."

"All right," he agreed immediately. "We'll make it to-morrow evening. That'll give you more time to think about it and give me your answer."

"What about pulling the old biddy's fat out of the fire?" she asked softly, unable to fling his words back into his face with quite the hostility she'd felt earlier.

His green eyes moved from the tip of her blond head, over slender curves, slowly down her long, tanned legs to brightly polished pink toenails. When his leisurely tour had finally returned to her eyes, he was smiling.

"This particular romance writer has not a single ounce of fat on her. So...how about it?"

Brandy shook her head, causing a honey-gold cloud to swirl between them. "Ryan, you're just succumbing to the mood of a delightful afternoon. You know as well as I do you weren't looking forward to meeting me any more than I was to meeting you. As for working together, a few hours ago you'd have gone fifteen rounds with one of the grizzlies at the zoo rather than work for five minutes with me."

"That was a few hours ago. Before I knew you."

"You don't know me."

How could he know her? How could anyone possibly know Brandy Raines? Even her name was a product of some stranger's imagination. There were times Brandy thought she was nothing more than a rather well-developed character.

"You're right," he agreed, a little too easily for comfort, Brandy thought. She was proved correct a moment later. "You've met my family, heard all the stories about me. Tomorrow night it'll be your turn. Do you have any relatives you'd like to invite to dinner? I'll pick up the check."

"That's a rather dangerous invitation." She managed a weak smile in an attempt to hide her disquiet at this particular line of conversation. "What if my family turns out to be the size of yours? You'd have to hire a hall."

"There's always hamburgers in the park." The dancing lights in his eyes encouraged acquiescence.

"Are you always this stubborn?"

"Always. How about you?"

"I've been called intransigent from time to time," she admitted.

"See all we have in common." The smile that had been hovering about the corners of his mouth split into a breathtakingly handsome grin. "I'll pick you up at eight."

"Eight-thirty," she corrected, giving in for now.

Brandy was too relieved with his apparent forgetfulness about her family to remain in his car any longer than necessary. She certainly couldn't relate the most painful aspects of her life with someone she'd never see again after tomorrow evening.

BRANDY HAD EVERY INTENTION of spending what was left of the afternoon working. As she curled up in the hammock in her backyard, *The Uninvited Corpse* in her hand, she planned simply to skim the text once again, interested only in proving to herself that their individual styles could never mesh.

Try as she might to keep her mind on her critical objective, Brandy soon found herself lost in the story. This time, Johnny Steele appeared to have taken on a new dimension. Still as arrogant and as chauvinistic as ever, he seemed to portray a more human, vulnerable side than he had before.

"Ridiculous," she muttered, slamming the paperback mystery shut. "You're just putting Ryan's personality on his hero."

That was no more soothing a notion as Brandy considered that, when she thought of Ryan, her body was infused with a certain warmth. It was more than just the fact he was good-looking, in an athletic, outdoorsy way. *That* she could handle without blinking an eye. California was overrun with such men. No, this feeling stemmed from something far different. Some inner premonition told her that if she allowed it, she could soon find herself caring very much for that pug-nosed cop-turned-author.

That idea was enough to make her decide she'd never be able to work with him. She glanced up at the clock; Maggie had closed her New York office long ago. Although she'd given Brandy her home telephone number, Brandy had never had a problem that couldn't wait until working hours. Until now. She located the number in her address book and punched the telephone buttons with unnecessary force.

"Maggie, I tried, but it just isn't going to work," she said the moment her agent answered.

"Brandy? Is that you?"

"It's me. And I know you've got my best interests at heart, but I really can't work with Ryan Sinclair," Brandy insisted.

There was a long silence as Brandy heard Maggie lighting a cigarette before exhaling a deep sigh. "What happened? Ryan's usually very nice; I can't think of anything he could have done to turn you off that fast."

"He was actually very nice," Brandy admitted. "When he wasn't coming off too much like Johnny Steele."

"Aha! So you *did* like him." When Brandy didn't answer, Maggie tried again. "Then what's the problem, as if I didn't already know?"

"I don't want to get involved with him, Maggie."

"We're only talking about collaborating on a book, not a lifetime commitment," Maggie pointed out dryly.

"It won't work."

"I see. And have you told him that?"

"I did. Several times."

"And?"

"And he refuses to listen."

Brandy couldn't help noticing that Maggie didn't sound at all surprised by Ryan's cheerful determination. "As your agent, may I ask where the matter stands now?"

"I'm not changing my mind," Brandy said firmly. "And I'm telling him that tomorrow night."

"Tomorrow night?"

"We're going to dinner," Brandy admitted, knowing how foolish she must sound.

"But you're not getting involved, right?"

"Right."

"How long have we worked together?" Knowing the question to be rhetorical, Brandy didn't answer. "Five years," Maggie continued, "and in all that time, I've never known you to have a serious relationship."

"Writing takes a lot of time and energy. I don't have any left to build a relationship," Brandy objected.

"Don't give me that," Maggie returned sharply. "You don't want any involvement because you're afraid of being hurt. That's the real truth, isn't it?" Her tone softened. "You don't have to answer that, Brandy—we both know I'm right." There was a little pool of thoughtful silence. "But I've never known you to feel like you have to run and hide from a man, either. What on earth did Ryan do to make you this afraid of him?"

"We cooked hamburgers for his family," Brandy answered nonsensically.

"All of them?" Maggie asked incredulously.

"There were enough Sinclairs in Chula Vista today to field two football teams," Brandy replied softly. "And although I honestly had a great time, I couldn't help comparing that huge, happy family with the way I grew up."

"So you're holding Ryan's family against him?"

Brandy shook her head, wishing she hadn't begun this conversation. She didn't know how to explain those unsettling feelings caused by the enjoyment she'd gotten from spending the afternoon with the Sinclair family.

The prevailing theory of foster care during Brandy's childhood had been against children remaining too long in any one home. It was felt that allowing them to become part of the family was disruptive when they had to leave to return to their own parents, or were adopted.

Although she'd prayed nightly for a miracle, Brandy's parents had never shown up to reclaim her, and her unorthodox situation had left her ineligible for adoption. By her twelfth birthday, she had lived in fourteen different homes. When she turned sixteen, she petitioned the court to declare her an emancipated minor, deciding that living on her own had to be better than the game of musical families she'd been playing all her life.

Oh, yes, Brandy thought, as she listened to Maggie listing all the professional reasons why she should collaborate with Ryan, she had learned the lesson against involvement early in life.

"I'm not changing my mind," she warned softly.

"But you are having dinner with him, aren't you?"

Brandy sighed. "I don't want to, but I think if I tried to back out now, the man would simply sit on my doorstep until I gave in. Or drag me screaming and kicking to the nearest restaurant."

"Ryan can be a little single-minded from time to time," Maggie admitted. "But I don't think he'd ever resort to force."

"That's what you think," Brandy muttered, remembering the way he'd dragged her out to the car today.

It was obvious Maggie wasn't going to be in her corner on this one, so Brandy wrapped up the conversation quickly, promising to keep her abreast of whatever she was working on. Then, knowing she was dabbling in masochism, she picked up Ryan's book, rereading it from cover to cover.

LATE THAT EVENING, Ryan rose from his desk, muttering a soft oath. He strode to the window, staring down at the foaming waves beating against the craggy La Jolla cliffs. He had scheduled the morning meeting with Brandy, the luncheon birthday party with Kevin, then six or eight hours of concentrated writing.

Even after he'd pressured Brandy into dinner, he thought he could shift into that state of consciousness that allowed the words to flow despite what was happening outside the glass walls. But he was unable to stop the thoughts that marched through his mind like a parade of busy ants.

Only his writing had saved him that year of Suzanne's death. He'd learned to put his depression away as he settled down for his stint at the typewriter. Over a period of months, Ryan found he could remember his wife in more happy times, and not as he'd last seen her.

After a period of mourning, followed by a time of healing, he'd begun seeing women again. Yet although he enjoyed their company, he'd never met another woman he wanted to share his life with. He'd successfully kept them on the fringes, delightful diversions who didn't interfere with his work or his mind.

Now, for some reason, Ryan was discovering that Brandy Raines had the ability to do exactly that. The heroine of his latest novel was voluptuous with sleek black hair and eyes that hinted at sensual secrets. But at the moment his mind continually turned up images of a tall, slender woman with wavy honey-colored hair and eyes as gently amber as a newborn fawn.

She wasn't behaving correctly, either. Instead of being a clinging vine, the heroine was fighting him, refusing to accept lines she felt outside the realm of her character.

"What in the hell do you know?" he muttered, looking over his shoulder at the black screen. "I'm the one who created you, dammit. I'm the one who knows what you'd say."

Even as he uttered the words, Ryan knew they were ridiculous. His heroine had taken on a life of her own, and it was unnervingly similar to the woman he hadn't been able to get out of his mind since driving back from Julian. Shaking his head, he returned to the word processor, flipped off the switch and left the house to take a long, solitary walk on the beach.

FIFTEEN MINUTES before Ryan was scheduled to arrive for dinner the following evening, Brandy stood in her slip, eyeing the contents of her closet.

"It's only a business dinner," she told herself firmly. "Not a date."

If that's the case, the unruly little voice in the far corner of her mind piped up, *why have you been trying on
clothes for the past two hours?* She glanced disparag-
ingly at the bed, which was covered with discarded ar-
ticles of clothing. Expelling a sigh of frustration, she
pulled out yet another selection, secretly admitting the
skirt and blouse were not exactly suitable for a business
dinner. Now, if this were a date...

RYAN STOOD on Brandy's front porch feeling inexplica-
bly like a kid on his first date. He couldn't remember the
last time he'd been this nervous. While he tried to tell
himself he was only concerned about Brandy's decision
on their collaboration, the excuse wasn't ringing quite
true, even to his own mind.

"Now *that's* what I call romantic," he said, the minute
she'd opened the door.

Brandy smiled, experiencing that warm glow once
again at the light of masculine appreciation gleaming in
Ryan's eyes.

"I'm sorry."

"For what?"

She brushed at nonexistent wrinkles on her skirt.
"Well, knowing how you feel about romance..." Her
tawny eyes were dancing with teasing lights.

Ryan could feel the fire kindling in his loins as he took
in the woman who seemed to have dressed to stir his
imagination. Had she known he'd spent all last night rereading *Love's Savage Embrace*, unable to separate the
heroine from the author?

The first time he'd skimmed the unabashedly romantic book, he'd mistakenly viewed the woman as a soft,
submissive individual. But with honest insight, Ryan
had, upon closer observation, noted a certain fatalistic

strength. The only reason Brandy's heroine had ac-
quiesced to that pirate rascal, Adam Black, was that she
admitted to her own sensual needs and chose not to ignore them for the sake of propriety. She was a perfect
match for the hero: her gentleness had softened his rough
edges, and her fiery determination had equaled his own.

Brandy could have stepped from the pages of her
novel, her ruffled, high-necked blouse fashioned of lace
that looked as if it had been dipped into tea. A cameo
rested over her pulse spot, and as Ryan's eyes lingered
there, Brandy could feel her blood quicken in response.

As a modern touch, her slim dark skirt ended below
the knee, hiding the scrape of yesterday's racket-ball
game, but displaying an attractive length of curved calf.
Her high heels put her almost at eye level with Ryan as
their gazes met and held.

"I've been thinking about you," he admitted in an un-
usually husky tone.

"About us writing together?"

With a display of reluctant honesty, Ryan shook his
head, causing a chestnut curl to fall over his forehead. In
the amber reflection of her porchlight, his dark hair appeared to be full of bright golden strands. Strands that
Brandy felt an inexplicable urge to sift through her fingers.

"No. Not writing."

"Oh."

They remained there, eyes engaged in a sensual little
dance for an indefinable length of time. It could have
been a moment, an hour or an eternity that Brandy and
Ryan shared in mute awareness. Unnerved by the silent
exchange taking place, Brandy couldn't repress her slight
shiver.

"You've got cool nights up here," he said softly, his words revealing that although his eyes had not left hers for a heartbeat, he'd been aware of her tremor.

"It's one of the things I like best about Julian."

"I know what I like best about Julian."

Brandy's answer caught in her throat as her mouth went suddenly dry. She licked her lips unconsciously, realizing her mistake as Ryan's eyes turned to emerald fire.

"I thought about you, too," she admitted finally.

"About us writing together?"

"That. And other things."

"Let's hear it for those other things," he murmured provocatively.

Ryan realized it was a dangerous game they were playing, and tried to remind himself he was here to convince Brandy that a collaboration would benefit both of them—not to carry her into that sunshine yellow room and ravish her on the bright melon couch.

"Perhaps we were both unduly influenced by each other's book," she ventured, trying to find a logical reason why she'd spent the night dreaming of a certain pirate who'd borne an unsettling resemblance to Ryan Sinclair.

"Perhaps that's it," Ryan agreed. Then, as Brandy's words sank in, he arched a dark brow. "I thought you didn't like Johnny Steele."

Brandy smiled, shrugging lace-covered shoulders. "I reread *The Uninvited Corpse* yesterday. I'll admit he grows on you..." Her lips quirked at the corners as her soft, feminine smile became a gamine grin. "I thought you didn't like Megan Fairfield," she said, referring to the heroine of *Love's Savage Embrace*.

"She's okay," Ryan admitted carelessly.

Brandy held her ground. "Just okay?"

"So she's terrific," he said, laughing, smoothing over the uncomfortable moment they'd been sharing. "And you're a talented writer, Brandy. That's why I'm going to do my damnedest tonight to convince you that we're a team made in heaven."

HEAVEN, BRANDY THOUGHT as they lingered over coffee. The entire evening had been absolutely heavenly. The food had been mouthwatering, Ryan's charm irrepressibly enjoyable, his tales of growing up in a house filled with children sounding as alien, yet every bit as wonderful, to Brandy as the fairy tales she'd loved as a child.

Ryan hadn't once brought up their proposed collaboration, and although Brandy knew she should just come out and tell him she wasn't going to work with him, she also was in no hurry to end what had been a delightful dinner. She held her tongue, promising herself to break the news to him. Soon.

"You must have been spoiled rotten," she suggested instead, considering the idea of Ryan's seven older sisters.

"I probably was," he admitted cheerfully. "Perhaps that explains why I hate not getting my own way, even now."

Brandy noticed that he accepted his tenacity as easily as he might accept possessing thick chestnut hair and green eyes. And rightfully so, she decided, thinking the trait seemed to be running through his veins, right along with his blood.

"Where do they all live?" She knew she'd met a great number of relatives yesterday afternoon, but couldn't place everyone.

"Uh-oh. If I'd known we were having a pop quiz to-night, I'd have brought my crib notes.... Let's see, Alice lives with her husband, a major in the air force, in Germany. Sarah lives here in San Diego, as do Annie, Jenny and Elizabeth. Laurie is married to a rancher living somewhere on the plains of Montana. I've never been there, but she swears it's heaven on earth."

Ryan smiled, obviously fond of that particular sister. "Julie joined the Peace Corps. In fact, as we sit here in sheer blissful comfort, dining on *nouvelle cuisine*, my sister is in darkest Africa, digging for ants with a pointed stick."

"It's chimpanzees who do that."

"Oh...well, I only hope she watches and learns. It might be the only food she gets." He grinned. "Julie's a pediatrician and the only one of the seven who isn't smugly, happily married. She felt working in a suburban clinic wasn't challenging enough so she filled out fifty-seven forms, got so many shots her arms looked like Swiss cheese, gave her Saks clothing to the other six and took off to do her Dr. Schweitzer thing."

"Amazing."

His eyes were warm and friendly. "She is. You'd like her. And she'd like you. You're both that terrific combination of gentleness combined with a streak of steel."

Brandy could feel the warmth darkening her skin to a deep apricot tone as Ryan successfully detoured the conversation to the more personal. She deftly turned it back to his family.

"It must have been wonderful growing up in that family." She was unable to keep the wistful note from her soft voice.

"It was noisy," he replied. "But my house is so damn quiet, I look forward to afternoons like yesterday. I like getting out with the kids." He grinned. "Even if Kevin does possess lousy timing."

"That's funny," she murmured half to herself, but Ryan caught her words.

He observed her over the rim of his cup as he took another drink of coffee. "What's funny?"

Brandy didn't want to admit she'd always dreamed of having a large family to make up for the one she'd never had as a child.

"Nothing, really." She traced a pattern on the tablecloth.

He observed her gravely. "Did I say something to make you unhappy?"

Brandy's attention returned to Ryan with a jolt. "Of course not. You've been the soul of discretion," she admitted in a surprised, but admiring tone.

"Then why the wistful look?"

"I was just thinking about your family." Brandy decided it wouldn't harm matters to tell him that much, at least.

"What about them?"

Ryan realized the Sinclair clan was a bit overwhelming to most people. It hadn't fazed Suzanne; they'd been childhood sweethearts, and she'd practically grown up as one more member of the household. He'd always considered his close and loving family an asset, but now was forced to view it in a more critical fashion. Could some women find it a liability? And more important, could Brandy Raines feel that way?

"There are quite a few of them," she remarked with a smile.

"That there are," Ryan affirmed, but the statement sounded more like a question to her ears, and Brandy knew he wasn't about to allow the subject to drop easily.

"And they're very nice."

"I think so," he agreed smoothly, his level gaze holding hers.

Brandy found herself enmeshed in an emerald trap. She remembered what he'd said yesterday, about wanting her to share something intensely personal with him. She had the feeling Ryan had decided the time had come.

"Tell me about yours," he suggested, his eyes not yet releasing hers.

"Mine?"

Don't ask, she pleaded inwardly.

"Your family," Ryan explained patiently, knowing Brandy was stalling, but not understanding why.

Suddenly an unpleasant thought occurred to him. God, what if she were married? She wasn't wearing a wedding ring, but the lack of a ring was unreliable evidence, even for a woman. There hadn't been any sign of a man about her house, but he certainly hadn't been invited into Brandy's bedroom.

Married women, as a rule, didn't have the freedom to go to parties one day, then dinner the next, without advance warning, Ryan assured himself. But a nagging little voice reminded him that husbands had been known to take business trips, too. Or even worse, perhaps she and her husband shared what was referred to as a "modern marriage," each allowed to play around. That was definitely the most distasteful thought of the batch.

Whatever the reason, Brandy Raines was stalling, attempting to come up with an acceptable answer to a question that should have been a cinch. Ryan didn't like it. Not one little bit.

"Are you finished?" he asked suddenly.

Startled by Ryan's suddenly gritty tone, Brandy lifted her cup, taking a last, quick gulp of cold coffee. "I am now."

The waitress had departed long ago, taking her copies of the charge slip, apparently realizing the couple wanted to linger uninterrupted. Ryan pushed his chair back with a brusque motion and rose to tower over her.

"Then there's no point in hanging around this place any longer, is there?" he asked with a flinty tone that reminded Brandy more of Johnny Steele.

"I suppose not."

Ryan stepped back, allowing her to walk ahead of him to the car. Brandy was bothered that she had no idea what had altered the pleasant mood. And even more disturbing was the fact that she cared so very badly.

"Where are we going?"

Ryan had not turned the car back toward Julian, but was instead headed in the direction of the coast.

"La Jolla."

"What's in La Jolla?"

"My place."

"I didn't agree to that," she protested.

"Tough." Now *that* was Johnny Steele.

"Ryan Sinclair, this is the second time you've abducted me and I'm not going to stand for it! Do you hear me?" She glared at him, arms folded across her lace-covered breasts.

"I hear you." He didn't take his eyes from the road.

"Then turn this car around right now."

He arched a rakish brow, granting her his attention for a split second. "On the freeway? Do you have any idea the fine I could get for that? Even if I could pilot this car across the median?"

He had a point. Although disinterested in the state of his bank account, Brandy offered an alternate solution.

"There's an off ramp up ahead, Ryan. I'd suggest you take it."

He shook his head, not removing his foot from the accelerator. "No way, lady. You've still got a promise to keep."

"I never promised to go to your house."

"Ah, but you did promise to discuss collaboration. Something we still haven't done," he pointed out with maddening accuracy.

"Which is just as well," she snapped. "Because I'd never work with anyone who'd behave in such an overbearing manner."

"And I wouldn't work with a liar," he retorted, his gaze censorious as it jerked from the freeway to rake her face.

Brandy's mind was instantly expunged of even the most futile answer to such an overwhelming accusation. She simply stared at Ryan as he returned his attention to the driving.

5

THE HOMES PERCHED on the cliffs of La Jolla were arranged in stair-step fashion, utilizing the valuable land in the most efficient means possible. As Ryan turned the Porsche into the driveway at the top of the cliff, Brandy stared, mentally comparing his house to her turn-of-the-century home in the mountains. Johnny Steele had obviously paid for it; no honest cop in the country could have afforded the mortgage payments on the attached three-car garage, let alone this magnificent house.

"I know." Ryan's voice was tinged with amusement. "It's not exactly your average beach cottage."

"It's not even your average beach castle. My God, Ryan, this place could spawn a year's worth of sermons on conspicuous consumption and not even get past the living room."

He laughed. "It's not as bad as it looks once you get inside," he promised. "In fact, you'll probably find it badly in need of a woman's touch. Come on in and I'll show you the story outline I've worked up."

He opened the hand-carved door that must have towered twenty feet above her head and pocketed the key. If the outside of Ryan's home screamed wealth, the inside was a jolt to the senses. Barely furnished, a few random pieces of furniture looked rather forlorn in rooms large enough to house a professional football stadium. Befitting the splendor of the setting, the ocean wall was glass, allowing a view unparalleled anywhere in the world.

"It's beautiful, Ryan," Brandy whispered, walking to the window and looking down on the whitecaps as they hit against the uplifted cliffs. The moon had tinged a silvery path on the black satin waters.

"It is, isn't it?" he said, coming up behind her. "You've no idea how much time I spend just staring out these windows. There's a magnitude to the Pacific that refuses to allow life's petty problems to seem the least bit significant."

Brandy nodded, a lump forming in her throat as she considered how often he must gaze out over the vast expanse of blue, remembering his wife and wishing she were here with him.

"Hey." Ryan's fingers cupped her shoulders, turning her toward him. His green gaze held hers with quiet insistence. "Don't create problems that don't exist, Brandy. I've already told you that I'm over Suzanne's death. I've been through all the psychologically acceptable stages and can honestly assure you that anything I'm feeling for you has nothing to do with her."

Was this man psychic? He seemed to realize that Brandy felt like an interloper in his home, as if it should be his wife standing with him right now, and not her.

Suzanne. The name brought up a small, delicate individual, gentle as a newborn kitten. Certainly not someone who'd crash into walls during racket-ball games or play football in the park. Brandy stifled a slight sigh, reminding herself that she'd sworn not to get involved with Ryan Sinclair in the first place. So what did she care that she was not at all his type?

"You were going to show me your outline," she suggested in a firm, impersonal tone. Although she had no intention of collaborating with him, it wouldn't hurt to see what he'd done so far.

Ryan's eyes narrowed with frustration. For someone who poured out her heart onto the pages of her novels,

Brandy Raines lived behind parapets made of stone. Every time she began to display a little honest emotion, she'd catch herself and back off, leaving him facing that damn wall. He wanted to know her.

He wanted to know what made her laugh, what made her cry, and yes, what it would be like to make her throw away her carefully created reserve and cry out with unleashed passion. Despite the way she kept pulling back from him, Brandy's writing displayed a dizzying range of emotions. He wanted to be the man to set them free.

Ryan's slight sigh echoed Brandy's as he decided returning the conversation to work would be the only way to keep her there.

"I'll get you the outline," he said, reluctantly taking his fingers from her shoulders. "Would you like anything to drink?"

Brandy shook her head. She could still feel the touch of Ryan's fingertips warming her skin, sending effervescence bubbling through her like sparkling champagne. No, she needed no spirits to amplify those sensations.

"No, thanks. I'm fine."

More than fine, he agreed inwardly as he left the room to retrieve the outline from his office.

"How in the world can you find anything?" Brandy had given up waiting and searched him out, watching in honest awe as he dug through the papers strewn over his desk.

"It's one of life's daily challenges," he said with a grin.

"Why don't you have a cleaning person come in once a week?" Her wide amber eyes moved over the room, taking in the piles of manuscripts that had accumulated on every flat surface.

"I do," he answered absently, skimming several pages of text before discarding them carelessly aside.

"Whatever you're paying, Ryan, it's far too much. This room looks as if a hurricane has torn through it."

"I don't let her clean in here," he mumbled. Then his grin widened and he held up a sheaf of papers triumphantly.

"Found it!"

He tossed some papers onto the floor, clearing off a chair for Brandy as he handed her the outline. She curbed her temptation to criticize the careless action toward what could very well be important material, turning her attention to Ryan's synopsis for *Risky Pleasure*.

She could soon see where the mystery could very well accommodate a romance. The story of a model, returned home to take over management of her grandfather's thoroughbred farm, running into opposition from his loyal, longtime foreman was a natural for sensual fireworks. While currently the plot line revolved around the theft of Risky Pleasure, the farm's prize filly, Brandy felt the suspense could easily be worked into a subplot. When she expressed this opinion to Ryan, he stared at her, raking long fingers through his sun-brightened chestnut hair.

"Subplot? Hell, that's the plot, Brandy. That's the meat of the book."

"I see. And I suppose you've planned for the romance between Blair and Clint to be the small potatoes." She looked up at him defiantly.

"No...more like the dessert. I thought we'd keep it light and fluffy."

"Terrific. I'm talking about writing a novel and the man's working on a cookbook," she countered dryly. "There's no way a romance between those two could remain light. He's obviously just a horsey version of Johnny Steele and she's a strong, independent woman. There's bound to be fireworks from page one."

Ryan decided not to tell Brandy he'd planned that the model-turned-ranch-owner be far more acquiescent.

"You may have a point," he said instead, thinking that their relationship had been anything but smooth thus far.

"Does the fact that you're arguing mean you've decided to work with me on it?"

Brandy knew that collaborating with Ryan Sinclair would demand the patience of a saint, and no one had ever ventured that description of her. When deeply involved in her writing she tended to be obsessive and impatient. Ryan had demonstrated innumerable times over the past two days that he was no pushover himself.

Yet there was something in the odd-couple relationship of the hero and heroine that leaped from the pages of his outline, piquing her interest. Ryan had concentrated on the suspense aspect, naturally, and from what she could see, it was flawlessly plotted. Although she had no admiration for that reprobate Johnny Steele, and Ryan's gritty way with words drove her up the wall, Brandy had to admit he was a master at the craft of pacing. The one element of the book he hadn't developed was the obvious opportunity for romance between Blair and Clint.

"All right," she agreed, handing him back the sheaf of rather crumpled white papers. "You've got yourself a partner."

The satisfied flash of those perfect white teeth gave Brandy the disconcerting impression that Ryan had never expected any other outcome.

"Thank you." He nodded in an oddly formal gesture. "Shall we toast our project?"

"One drink," she said. "Then I'm going home. I've got to get to bed early if I'm going to be ready to work when you show up tomorrow morning."

A chestnut brow climbed the tanned expanse of forehead, and Ryan's fingers froze on the wire covering the champagne cork. He'd chilled the sparkling wine this afternoon, fully expecting to come out the victor in the little game he and Brandy had been playing. But she'd just thrown him a curve.

"*I* show up? Do you mean in Julian?"

Brandy's eyes widened. "Of course."

"I thought we'd work here."

"I'm unaccustomed to working in a pigsty, Ryan."

"It's creative clutter," he protested instantly. There was challenge in his tone, as well as a warning. A warning she chose to ignore.

"It's trash," she countered, picking up a tip sheet and waving it in his face.

Ryan yanked it from her hands, flinging it in the direction of the desk behind him. Missing the target, the paper fluttered unheeded to the floor.

"That's research."

She arched a challenging blond brow. "Research?"

"Research. How the hell do you think I could write a racing book if I didn't study handicapping?"

Damn. Chalk one up for the home team. "Oh," she said with exaggerated disinterest. "But I still won't work here, Ryan. Look at this mess." Her gaze raked over the scattered piles of books and papers.

"I need the ocean," he argued. "When I get blocked I watch the waves. They never fail to relax my thoughts."

So don't get blocked, Brandy felt like retorting. Instead she forced her mind to come up with a more logical suggestion.

"Why don't you work here and I work in Julian? We can get together periodically and iron out any problems."

"No way. If I'm going to collaborate, lady, I want us working together as a team. And teams aren't two independent operators shoving mismatched texts into an unworkable whole."

Brandy recognized iron-willed stubbornness when she saw it, possessing a fair share herself. She decided not to point out that she knew several writing teams who managed to work apart and turned out marvelous novels.

"Then *you* come up with a solution," she retorted.

Ryan noted her determination and knew compromise was in order. He'd refereed enough conflicts in the streets to know that total victory was nice, but not often possible. Damn, she was stubborn!

"We'll work one day in Julian, one day here."

"That wouldn't work. We'd spend half our lives driving back and forth on the San Diego freeway system, Ryan."

"All right. I have another solution." He began twisting at the champagne cork once again, obviously deciding to bring this conversation to a close.

"What's that?" Brandy eyed him warily.

"You move in here for the first week and I'll move into your house the second. If we keep to a rotating schedule, we'll only be commuting one day a week."

Live under the same roof with the alter ego of Johnny Steele? The man must think she had a screw loose.

"We'll do it one day at a time," she stated, grabbing one of the glasses to catch the bubbling gold liquid spurting from the bottle.

Ryan lifted his glass to hers, the crystal ringing like a silver bell as they touched rims. Well, it had been a nice fantasy, he thought. But probably too loaded with potential problems to ever succeed.

"Agreed. Here's to collaboration, Brandy. In the fullest sense of the word."

Brandy felt her cheeks redden at the smooth insinuation in his deep tone and lowered her eyes to her glass. "To collaboration," she murmured, having the uneasy feeling she'd just flung herself off that cliff outside. She'd taken the leap, and from now on there was no turning back.

"YOU WERE TELLING me about your family." The soft tones broke into Brandy's study of the moon-gilded ocean. She realized that Ryan was right. The vastness of the pano-ramic scene seemed to calm the mind, allowing thoughts to float free.

She'd been given a tour of the house, finding that it was only Ryan's office that was in such a state of disorder. The remainder of the rooms, while as sparsely furnished as this, were neat and orderly. She hadn't missed the picture on the bedside table, a beautiful young woman smiling out of the silver frame, her eyes lit with love for the photog-rapher. Suzanne. Brandy had been surprised by the lance of pain that momentary glimpse had sent through her.

She'd weakened on her vow of a single glass of cham-pagne, finding that she was reluctant to have Ryan take her home. She'd never experienced the peace of mind she had discovered while sitting here beside him on the blue sofa, watching the waves carve away the coastline, as they had since the beginning of time.

"Was I?"

"Damn it, Brandy, how hard a question can that be?" He took her left hand, running his fingertips over the third finger. "Unless you're married, that is."

Brandy couldn't miss the question in Ryan's tone and yanked her hand away. "So that's why you called me a liar."

He didn't deny it. "Are you?"

She shook her head emphatically. "No."

"Then why the big secret? We're just talking about a family here, Brandy. It's no big deal. Everyone has one."

How easy it had been for him, Brandy thought scath-ingly. He'd grown up in the bosom of that huge family who loved and cared for him. Even his sister-in-law had dem-onstrated her concern yesterday when he'd injured his knee on that illegal tackle. How could he possibly understand?

"Not everyone, Ryan. I don't."

He was momentarily disconcerted, his green eyes searching for answers in her tight expression.

"I don't understand. Unless you've landed from a planet where the population is spawned in test tubes, sweetheart, it's a little difficult not to at least have parents."

Tell him, a self-protective little voice screamed. *Tell him the story about your family in Oregon. About the father who owns a hardware store and belongs to the Elks lodge and lives for trout fishing. Tell him about your mother who suffered a midlife crisis and is now happily selling real estate in the Willamette Valley. And your brother, the engineer living in Salem, who designs boxcars.*

The mythical family had been created with all the care and precision Brandy gave to the formulation of any of her fictional characters. She'd given them personalities, a charming old house and a varied assortment of pets. She'd used James and Caroline Raines whenever anyone possessed an interest in her family, and over the years there had been times the couple actually seemed real to her. But to her shock, Brandy heard the truth coming uncensored from her lips.

"I don't have any family, Ryan. I was abandoned as a baby and grew up in foster homes. I don't know anything about my mother or my father. I don't know if I have any sisters or brothers." She tipped her head back, finishing off the champagne. "Hell, I don't even know if Brandy Raines is my real name."

"Hey," he murmured, "that's nothing to be ashamed of."

She opened her mouth to protest that she was certainly not ashamed of her parentless state when the warm glow in his bright eyes rendered her speechless. Those orbs moved across her face with the intensity of a physical caress, and once again Brandy could feel a silvery net settling down about them.

"None of it matters, Brandy. Not my family, not your lack of family. Try to think of us as just two people who could make each other feel very, very good."

His words could have been right out of one of his novels. Persuasive, silky, they coaxed feminine acquiescence. They also brought reality slamming back down upon her. Brandy sat up, reminding herself she was a survivor. She'd overcome a lifetime of hardships by disallowing herself personal involvements. Every self-protective instinct she possessed told her that Ryan Sinclair was extremely hazardous.

"You don't write bad dialogue, Ryan. Is that one of Johnny Steele's more successful lines?"

"Nope, that's one of Ryan Sinclair's obviously less successful lines," he said with a laugh, rising reluctantly from the couch. "I suppose now you're going to insist I throw in the towel and take you home so you can be all bright-eyed and bushy-tailed for our first day working together."

"That's a good idea," she agreed. "It's late, and sunrise is coming earlier every morning."

"Sunrise?" Ryan stared at her.

Brandy nodded, rising to face him. "Sunrise," she confirmed. "I always get up with the sun."

His green eyes grew even wider, if that was possible. "I didn't realize I'd be working with a masochist. What in the world do you find to do at that ungodly hour?"

It was Brandy's turn to stare. "Write, naturally. What else would I be doing?"

He gave her a friendly leer. "I can think of a number of things, each and every one involving staying in bed."

"Well, unless you write in bed, Ryan, you're going to have to change your habits," she answered with a sweet smile, picking up her purse and heading toward the foyer.

He was right on her heels. "If you're talking about me putting words to paper before noon, forget it, lady. Because I won't do it."

As Brandy ducked under the arm holding the door open, she breathed in a deep gulp of salt-tinged air, exhaling it wearily. *Here we go again.* She wondered what had ever made her think a collaboration with Ryan Sinclair was remotely possible. They had absolutely nothing in common.

She waited to answer him until they were in the car. "Of course you'll do it, Ryan. When we work at my house, we work on my timetable...just as I'll work on your timetable at your house." Brandy gave herself points for throwing in a compromise position before Ryan could complain.

He slid her a mocking glance. "That will be a little difficult."

"Why?"

Ryan's tawny eyes moved over her features, from the defiant sparkle in her tawny eyes to her lips pursed in frustrated irritation to the stubborn tilt of her chin. The moonlight streaming through the windshield gave the appearance of midday, the illumination easily bright enough for him to view the determination etched into every line of that lovely face. For a while there, it looked as though this idea might work. Now he was convinced it had been the stupidest scheme he'd ever come up with.

"Because," he returned unequivocally, twisting the key in the ignition, "I write at night. Sometimes all night." He gave his statement time to sink in, then added with maddening logic, "Now, do you want to tell me how we can work all night on my days to set the schedule, then begin at dawn when it's your turn? Obviously one of us is going to have to alter his or her way of writing."

And she knew exactly who he had in mind. "Agreed."

Ryan gave her an appraising glance. "Really? You'll change your hours just like that?"

"Of course not. I was simply agreeing that one of us has to change."

"I already agreed to compromise and start at noon." A note of aggravation roughened his voice.

"That's fine for your days. On mine we begin at dawn."

"Ten," he countered.

"Seven."

"Nine."

"Seven-thirty and that's my last offer," Brandy insisted.

"May I point out that seven-thirty is a helluva lot closer to sunrise than noon? You're not even making an attempt to meet me halfway."

"All right, seven forty-five. But not one minute later."

"That's what you consider halfway?" he questioned in disbelief.

"It's as far as I'll go, Ryan. Take it or leave it," she announced, finality evident in her tone.

Brandy forced her gaze out the car window, afraid to chance a peek in his direction. *Take it*, she begged inwardly, wondering if, in her drive to maintain her independence, she'd managed to drive him away entirely. As much as she hated to admit it, she wanted very much to work with Ryan Sinclair. And honesty was making her face the fact that it had more to do with these strange feelings she had for the man than the fact that intuition told her they could write a very good book together.

Damn. Ryan flexed his fingers on the top of the steering wheel. No one, man or woman, had ever challenged him at every turn and gotten away with it. If Brandy Raines were any other writer, he would never have, for an instant, considered collaboration. He had always worked alone and liked it just fine, thank you.

The moment to call off the entire farce had been when she began negotiating *where* to work. By agreeing to compromise on that score, he'd opened the door to all sorts of outrageous demands. Now she was fighting him on *when* to work. Then there was the fact she'd given off unnerving hints of being none too keen on his story line and characterization.

If he had any sense, he'd call the whole deal off right now. But as much as he knew their working together was going to be like skydiving without a parachute, Ryan wanted to spend more time with her.

"You realize, of course, that you're making the Middle East peace talks look like child's play?"

"Take it or leave it," Brandy repeated with false bravado to the well of darkness outside the window.

He exhaled a sigh of weary resignation. "All right, seven forty-five every day, but we work two days in La Jolla for every one in Julian. Starting at my place tomorrow."

That was fair, she acknowledged, since she'd be up anyway, she might as well take on the additional commuting. It was an hour from her house to Ryan's with the best of traffic conditions. She knew if she forced him to fight rush-hour morning traffic when he preferred to be nestled in his nice warm bed with a willing woman, he'd be less agreeable to making the changes she viewed as necessary in his outline.

"Agreed."

The grin Brandy gave him was absolutely breathtaking, and Ryan knew that however painful the days of early awakening would be, the warmth of that smile suddenly made it all seem worthwhile.

"GOOD NIGHT." Ryan was standing on Brandy's front porch, staring at her mouth.

"Good night," she whispered, looking up at the emerald eyes, which were locked to her lips.

"Thank you for dinner."

"I think I'm supposed to say that to you," she murmured. Neither pair of eyes had moved.

"Then thank you for the company."

So that's all it was. Her lips curved downward in a disappointed frown. "You hate to eat alone," she diagnosed in a flat, accepting tone.

"I never did. Until tonight. I think you've managed to change a lifetime of eating habits."

He was making her so nervous, gazing at her lips with that steady intensity. Brandy caught her bottom lip between her teeth.

"Don't." His fingers brushed her lip, sparking it with dancing flames.

Brandy closed her eyes at the sensations such an innocent touch could bring, and Ryan, recognizing her shared need, moved his fingers to cup her chin.

Her eyes remained tightly shut, but Brandy waited, her heart in her throat for his dark head to lower and his lips to cover hers. Ryan didn't disappoint her as his tongue first lightly caressed the teeth marks on the soft skin of her bottom lip. Then his mouth moved seductively on hers, testing, teasing, then tasting more fully of her honeyed essence as his lips parted, coaxing hers to respond in kind. Ryan was rapidly finding that Brandy Raines had the ability to make him drunker than a flagon of robust port.

"I think this could be a very successful collaboration," he murmured against her lips.

"So do I," she agreed softly.

"How would you like our first day's work to be here?"

Brandy's eyes flew open and she stepped back in surprise. "Really?"

"Really."

Despite the undeniable enticement of his smile, Brandy didn't quite trust Ryan. "Why are you being so agreeable?"

"Well," he admitted, "I thought we might finish this farewell in more intimate surroundings." He reached out to gently pull her toward him. "Then, since I'd already be here when your beloved sun peeped over the horizon, it wouldn't make a lot of sense treking back across the valley."

That did it. "We'll do no such thing. And this farewell is most definitely finished, Ryan Sinclair!"

Brandy pulled away from him, the abrupt gesture causing Ryan to reach behind him for the intricately carved pillar of the porch railing. The resultant crack shattered the nighttime silence, and she looked over her shoulder just in time to see him take an out-of-control, backward somersault off the porch.

6

THE STRING OF EXPLETIVES hung in the fragrant country air as Ryan hit the ground with a dull thud.

"Are you all right?"

Brandy was with him in an instant, kneeling beside the outstretched male form, her hands moving over him like delicate birds, searching for broken bones.

"Brandy Raines, you're an absolute menace," he complained, the stars still circling his head dizzyingly. He struggled to sit up.

"No, Ryan, you've had a bad fall.... Let me help you," she offered in a soft, distressed tone. Brandy wrapped her arms around his shoulders, lowering her head at the exact moment Ryan's came up. The crash of foreheads caused lightning to flash behind his eyes. He fell back to the ground closing his lids against the waves of nausea.

"Damn!"

His initial exclamation was followed by another heated series of oaths, far more colorful, and if Brandy hadn't been so concerned about Ryan's physical well-being, she would have protested. As she viewed him lying there, unnaturally still, his lush brown lashes resting against ashen cheeks, Brandy forgot her own discomfort. She leaned over him once again, the fingers of her right hand brushing back the hair from his forehead while her left hand continued its exploration of his body.

"Ryan?" she whispered into the darkness. "Ryan, are you all right?"

She opened the buttons of his dress shirt with trembling fingers that pressed against the rippling muscles of his chest, probing for broken ribs. Ryan's resultant, muffled groan only served to increase her concern. He *had* broken something.

"Ryan, I'll go call an ambulance."

She breathed the message near his ear, not knowing if he was even aware of her words. Was he unconscious? Dear God, what if he had internal bleeding? She'd never forgive herself. Her hand traveled down across the flat of his abdomen, pressing delicately, not knowing how to determine the extent of his injuries.

His hand suddenly lifted from the ground to cover hers, holding it against his body.

"Don't go," he moaned.

"I have to," she protested softly. "You need help."

"I need you," he countered, moving their hands together until she was given vivid proof of that claim. Her startled gaze flew to his face, crashing into sparkling, devilish eyes.

"You big fake!" She pulled her hand away, glaring at him.

A dark brow arched on a forehead that now bore a darkening red imprint. "That's a bit difficult to fake, darlin'," he drawled, laughter deepening his velvety voice.

She leaped to her feet, her anger taking over, serving as a balm to her tormented nerves. Nothing had ever frightened her as much as the prospect of Ryan lying lifeless on her lawn.

"I was honestly worried sick about you, Ryan Sinclair, and all the time you've been having the time of your life, watching me make a damn fool of myself."

He raised himself up onto his elbows, his expression revealing disgruntled surprise. Brandy warned herself not to pay any heed to the rippling of his chest muscles, or the manner in which the soft material of his slacks hugged his flat stomach before drawing taut over the corded strength of his thighs.

Ryan's attitude was less than cordial as he shot her a fed-up look. "If there's anyone who's made a damn fool of himself, it's been me, Brandy. Every time I get within ten feet of you I end up wounded."

His lips twisted in a self-deprecating grin that failed to extend to his icy eyes. "Do you know that I survived nine years on the San Diego police force with fewer injuries than you've given me in the past two days? You're nothing but an accident just waiting to happen, lady."

Brandy stared at him in openmouthed astonishment. Her hand flew to the lacy bodice of her blouse.

"Me? I certainly didn't push you off the porch, Ryan."

"I don't remember jumping," he returned instantly.

Brandy lifted her shoulders in what she could only hope was an uncaring shrug. "I can't help it if you have a nasty tendency of throwing your weight around. Besides, it's an old house. You should expect things to be more fragile than that fortress you've built for yourself."

Ryan looked past her to the broken railing. "Why in the hell don't you keep this place in decent repair so your guests aren't in danger of breaking their necks?"

That was a low blow. Brandy loved her eighty-year-old house and was continually pouring money into upgrading the ancient plumbing system, the wiring, which the fire department had declared definitely hazardous, and a roof that leaked in a new spot every time it rained. It seemed that as soon as she took care of one domestic emergency, another popped up to take its place.

"Guests are *invited*, Ryan. You weren't," she reminded him, squaring her shoulders.

Ryan muffled a low oath as he struggled to his feet, trying not to groan as every bone in his body protested. "You weren't complaining a few minutes ago," he pointed out. "Before that little act of assault and battery." He managed a crooked smile of absolution. "You're turning out to be a very dangerous woman, Brandy Raines."

His fingers cupped her shoulders, massaging a sensuous message. *You're the dangerous one, Ryan Sinclair,* Brandy argued silently. *Because I don't know how to protect myself against you. Against these feelings.*

Viewing her apparent distress, Ryan lightly touched the red bump on her forehead. "Did you hurt yourself when we knocked heads?"

"Not too badly," she whispered, moved, in spite of herself, by his concern. "How about you?"

Ryan shrugged carelessly. "I'll be okay." His eyes suddenly lit with devilish insinuation. "Want to go inside and check each other out for hidden injuries?"

"You're doing it again," she objected. "Behaving like a character from one of your books."

Ryan exhaled a light, accepting sigh. "You realize that you're only going to disappoint us both."

"I'm not disappointed."

"I'm not talking about you." His lips quirked with a suppressed smile.

"Then who?"

"The first is one admittedly frustrated mystery writer. The other soon-to-be-disappointed individual is your neighbor." He tilted his head in the direction of the house next door.

Brandy's gaze followed his, seeing the unmistakable silhouette of Mrs. Simpson against the lacy curtains. "Oh no," she groaned.

"Hey, you weren't doing anything to be ashamed of, Brandy. Although I'd never have guessed you'd be one of those kinky women who gets off on beating up your men before making love to them. Next time, shall I bring along my handcuffs?"

He waggled his eyebrows in a friendly, lusty movement Brandy had described in novels, but always secretly considered a physical impossibility.

Her fury exploded and without thinking, she swung at him, aiming for that mouth curved into a teasing, masculine smirk.

With lightning speed, Ryan ducked, the air whistling over his head.

"Hey, it was just a suggestion," he protested, catching both her hands and holding them harmless far from her body.

Brandy glared at him. "Do you realize that you're absolutely disgusting when you slide into that Johnny Steele personality?"

Ryan surprised her by smiling, his expression one of amusement. "Really?" he inquired, his thumbs brushing the inside of her wrists.

Mentally issuing an apology to her orthodontist, Brandy ground her nearly straightened teeth together and shot him a quelling glance.

"Really," she confirmed. "And if you don't let go of me right now, Ryan, that knee will have a brand-new injury."

He ignored her threat, giving her a tantalizing grin. "You wouldn't want to do that, Brandy."

"Yes, I would. And I will, I swear, Ryan," she spat back between clenched teeth. The damage she was doing to-night would require her to wear her retainer for six additional months.

He moved her arms behind her back, effectively bringing their bodies together. Every muscle Brandy possessed tensed in response as his chest flattened her breasts, his belly pressed against the soft swell of her abdomen and his thighs met hers with a masculine insistence.

"Don't swear, darlin'," he murmured as he expertly slid the uninjured knee between hers. "It's not at all ladylike."

Brandy bucked against the hard warmth of his body, finding that Ryan possessed the superior strength. All she succeeded in doing was creating an unnerving heat between them, like twigs rubbed together to kindle a fire.

"Let go of me," she choked out, the words ragged as his kisses trailed sparks up her neck.

"You don't want that," he argued in a throaty murmur, his lips plucking at the soft skin just above the ivory cameo.

She swallowed hard. "I do."

He pulled his head back, eyeing her thoughtfully. "If I let go of you, will you run away?"

"Yes," she insisted.

As Ryan slowly released her hands, Brandy was appalled to find herself trapped by her desire for this man.

"You wouldn't run," he whispered, his palms framing her face as he held her gaze to his.

Brandy longed to lie, but knew there was no point. "No," she admitted softly. "I wouldn't run."

Ryan's fingers trailed down her throat, where he could feel the wild heartbeat under the cameo, resembling that of a frightened bird. "But you're afraid." He pulled his head back, a softness in his eyes she'd not seen before.

Brandy couldn't answer.

"You're afraid," he repeated in a harsh whisper, this time no question in his tone. "Are you really afraid of me, Brandy? Or of yourself?"

"I don't know," she managed to get out.

Ryan looked at her for a long time, saying nothing as his somber gaze moved over her face. He shook his head, the dark strands seeming to scatter gold dust in the muted glow of the moonlight.

"All right, sweetheart. We'll play this your way. For now," he added, chagrin etched into every line of his tanned face. "Because when we make love, Brandy, I want you to want it as badly as I do."

Ryan was limping back down her sidewalk before Brandy could answer. "Good night, sweetheart. I'll see you at my place at seven forty-five."

His words cut through her sensual lassitude. "Your place? I thought you'd offered to work here tomorrow."

He flashed her that devilishly attractive grin. "I did. But if you remember correctly, my argumentative romance writer, you turned me down. So, tomorrow we write our prose to the evocative sound of crashing waves instead of crickets."

Brandy watched as he climbed into the sleek Porsche and took off in the direction of La Jolla. When she could no longer view the illumination of the red taillights, she entered her house. The grandfather clock gonged fifteen minutes past the hour, and cutting a glance to the oak case, Brandy groaned as she realized it was already after two. Why had she been the one to insist on beginning so damn early?

As she drifted off to sleep, her only consolation was that at least she was a morning person. Ryan, on the other hand, would probably be dead when she showed up in a few hours on his doorstep. But in her dreams, the overwhelmingly virile man was anything but exhausted.

RYAN PACED the Mexican tile flooring of his vast home, walking a marathon distance before daybreak. He'd tried unsuccessfully to sleep, his mind obsessed with the problem of Brandy Raines. Rising from the rumpled sheets, he'd gone into his office, finding work also an impossibility.

He'd been trying to pinpoint the feeling he had for Brandy all night, and the only thing he could come up with was ridiculous. For love, the streetwise, pragmatic ex-cop told himself, did not come like a lightning bolt from a clear blue California sky. It grew slowly, nourished by tender care over the years.

Love made you feel wonderful, on top of the world, capable of achieving the most miraculous of feats. Love did not make you feel as if you were sinking into quicksand.

But, he admitted, twisting the shower knobs with a vicious gesture, if this wasn't love, then he'd be damned if he understood what in the hell it could be.

He was still considering that problem when the deep sounds of the front door chimes interrupted his shower. Throwing on a pair of cutoffs, he ran to the door, flinging it open to Brandy.

"Good morning!" he welcomed her, unreasonably happy to see her again.

Brandy stared at the man framed in the tall doorway. For someone who professed to be a night person, Ryan Sinclair looked disgustingly chipper this morning. His smile was absolutely brilliant, making her once again experience a stab of sheer envy for such gorgeous teeth. If the man ever suffered permanent writer's block, he could make a fortune doing toothpaste commercials.

Deepening lines fanned out attractively from green eyes issuing a warm welcome. Brandy determined that he couldn't have been up all that long since his chestnut hair glistened with the moisture from a recent shower. Tiny droplets of water nestled like diamonds in his chest hair, and she had to fight down the impulse to tangle her fingers in the curling mat.

"Good morning," she answered.

She gave him a polite smile, entering the house, trying not to reveal the jolt of desire imparted by the spicy soap scent that clung to his skin. Why couldn't the man have taken time to put on a shirt before answering the doorbell?

"Want some coffee?" he asked with inordinate cheeriness.

"I'd love a cup."

"It's on the counter in the kitchen." He pointed toward a doorway. "Go ahead and help yourself while I finish dressing."

Brandy forced a casual glance at the vibrantly attractive male clad only in a pair of cutoff jeans. His long legs were graced with the same dark hair of his chest, and Brandy suffered a quickening in her middle regions as she imagined those legs tangled with hers, in the manner they'd been so vividly depicted in her dreams. One thing she hadn't imagined was the network of scars crossing his knee, a road map of the pain he'd suffered.

Even with that flaw to his perfection, Ryan's body managed to surpass the man who'd tormented her sleep. Tanned to the color of teak, he possessed a sleek physical beauty he seemed to take for granted as he stood before her, amazingly casual in his near nudity.

"That's a good idea," she remarked with a calmness she didn't feel, jerking her eyes from the dark arrow of fine body hair disappearing below his belt.

"Are you sure about that?" His grin was suggestive, echoed by the mischievous glint in his eyes. "If you had as hard a time sleeping as I did, perhaps we should reschedule our work and go back to bed."

"Good try, Steele," she returned, answering the man's alter ego, who had just made an appearance. "But I'm not interested."

Brandy was treated to a boyishly startled expression. "Really? Not at all?"

"Really. Not at all." It crossed Brandy's mind that she had probably lied more in the past couple of days than she had all year.

"Most women are more than a little interested," he offered, as if she'd find some appeal in belonging to the majority. If anything it only strengthened her resolve not to allow this blatantly seductive man to chip away any further at her already eroding willpower.

"Look here," she protested firmly, "we've got to get one thing straight if we're going to work together."

"You're going to insist we don't make love," he predicted, the smile on his face not fading one bit in wattage.

"That's it."

She nodded her honey blond head firmly, holding his gaze with sheer determination. Her strength wavered slightly as she took in the dark lashes that framed his warm green eyes so enticingly, but then she moved her study to his upturned lips. There was something about Ryan Sinclair's smile that was so devastatingly beautiful it only served to irritate her. No one person should be so lucky.

Brandy was surprised when Ryan laughed, a husky deep-chested sound. "Well, that's one problem out of the way," he said, flashing her one more brilliant grin before turning to leave the room.

Brandy reached out to stop him, finding his state of undress a distinct disadvantage as she was forced to latch onto his waistband. Her fingers inadvertently slid between his warm skin and the soft denim, failing to come into contact with any material in between. Good Lord, she realized weakly, he wasn't wearing anything under the cutoffs.

"Change your mind?" he asked on a friendly note, which assured her he'd be totally accommodating to anything she might suggest.

"I just want to know what you find so funny about my wanting to keep this on a working basis."

Ryan shook his head, a low chuckle punctuating his words. "That wasn't it. I just spent all night trying to figure out how to tell you the same thing."

"Oh."

It came as an oddly unpleasant surprise to Brandy that Ryan didn't want to make love to her, after all. She was certain the man was not that choosy in his female companionship; his blatantly masculine attitude just screamed seduction. Then there were all those escapades with Johnny Steele. She wondered how many of them were nothing but thinly disguised autobiographical sexual interludes.

"Oh," he mimicked, a sensual smile hovering about his lips. "Don't tell me you're disappointed?"

"Of course not," she protested.

"Good." He gave her an innocent look. "Then perhaps you'll unhand me so I can finish getting dressed."

She'd forgotten all about her fingers clutching his wasitband. Brandy's hands flew from Ryan's body as if burned. Damn the man! She could cheerfully strangle him without a moment's guilt. Ever since Maggie had first come up with the crazy idea of her collaborating with Ryan, her life had turned to absolute chaos.

Having been dealt a life without a single thread of stability, Brandy had developed remarkable self-control. Legally on her own since her sixteenth birthday, she'd been emotionally independent since birth. Yet Ryan Sinclair was quite effectively demolishing all the self-restraint she'd acquired over the years, steamrollering over her with a smooth, velvet strength.

She couldn't work with him and protect herself, as well, she realized. While Brandy was totally unfamiliar with what the man was doing to her heart, she knew instinctively he was capable of turning her life upside down.

"I can't work with you," she whispered, turning away to stare out at the pounding surf. The fog still had a hold on the land, blanketing them in a misty gray veil.

The teasing smile disappeared from Ryan's face. He came to stand behind her. Neither spoke as they watched the tides carve away at the rugged cliffs. A lone beachcomber walked along the dampened sand, barely visible in the fog, picking up shells left by the receding water.

"I can't work without you," he said, finally breaking the silence.

Brandy turned, knowing as she did so that she'd be a goner. She was proved right as she lifted her gaze the few inches to his eyes. There was no longer any laughter dancing in his eyes as he surveyed her with great gravity.

"Of course you can." Brandy remained statue still, unable to flee from the intensity of Ryan's gaze.

"I need you, Brandy."

"You've already stated you have lots of women, Ryan. You don't need me."

Ryan ran an impatient hand down the back of his head. "I've never had any problem finding women to take to bed, Brandy, but what we have here is a more basic problem. One of survival."

She arched a honey brow, inviting elaboration.

"Eating. And paying the rent," he tried to explain, not quite understanding any of this himself. He jammed his hands into the back pockets of his cutoffs, preventing his fingers from tangling in her silken hair as they yearned to do.

Brandy's attention was drawn by the brusque gesture to his hips, where the soft, faded denim was pulling tightly across his body. Oh Lord, how did either of them think they were going to get any work done?

"I still don't understand." Her voice was weak, totally unlike her own.

"I'm in trouble with my heroine," he admitted, the tightly bunched muscles of his jaw clearly exhibiting his displeasure. "I'm having a helluva time getting a feel for her. I need you, Brandy…or I'll end up pitching six weeks' hard work."

A ray of sun cut through the fog outside the window, illuminating Ryan's features, casting shadows from his long lashes across the planes of his face. His eyes were directed downward, toward the floor, and it was impossible to divine what he was thinking.

Was it possible Ryan Sinclair truly needed her creative input? Brandy didn't know whether to be pleased that he considered her valuable as a collaborator, or depressed that he found her expendable as a bed partner. She sighed, wondering, not for the first time certainly, about her atypical vacillation.

Ryan mistook the small exhalation of breath as refusal. His hands left his pockets to touch her waist, his fingers pressing into her skin. All guard had fallen away from his eyes as he squinted against the bright sun.

"Don't turn me down, Brandy...please?"

"Please? That's not a word you toss around, Ryan." Not from what she'd seen so far, anyway.

"I know. I save it for the really important stuff."

At that moment, viewing his somber green eyes, Brandy wondered how she'd ever be able to refuse this man anything.

"I'll stay," she agreed, swallowing hard on the lump in her throat. "Although I'm surprised you'd want to work with me, since you seem to think I'm a walking disaster area."

Oh, you're a disaster, all right, Brandy Raines, Ryan considered with fatal resignation. His life had irrevocably altered when Maggie had thrown him together with this exceptionally lovely, strong-willed romance writer. And while the thought of working with Brandy stirred his blood, it also scared the living daylights out of him. And not because he was worried about breaking his neck. It was his heart that had suddenly been placed in danger.

"I'll just have to remember to keep up the payments on my insurance." He gave her a crooked smile. "I'd better get dressed," he suggested.

She nodded. "Good idea. I'll pour some coffee. Would you like something to eat?"

His face brightened. "Did you bring something with you?"

"No. But I'm capable of scrambling a couple of eggs," she volunteered.

"That'd be great. If I had any," he tacked on with an obvious display of disappointment.

"You get dressed, Ryan. I'll see what I can find in your kitchen."

His expression did not display a great deal of hope. "Good luck."

Brandy allowed herself the honest pleasure of watching him leave the room, his lean hips moving with an almost feline grace as he walked. There was no sign of his limp today, and although she'd refused to accept any responsibility for that accident last night, or his injury during that ridiculous tackle, she was glad he'd suffered no permanent damage.

"You're right." Brandy eyed him over the rim of her cup as he entered the kitchen a few minutes later. No wonder it was so clean. Obviously the man's only domestic chore was that of making coffee.

"What am I right about this time?"

She chose to ignore the teasing masculine arrogance in his deep tone.

"The fact that all you have in your refrigerator is a six-pack of Coors, half a salami and two slices of pepperoni pizza that are busily growing their own penicillin culture."

"I didn't think you'd have much luck," he agreed.

"You're awfully cheerful for a man who's going to go without breakfast."

"No problem—we'll stop and pick something up on the way."

Brandy felt a familiar premonition skim up her spine. She'd already determined that Ryan was the most intransigent when he brought out that dazzling smile.

"On the way? On the way where?"

"To Glorietta Bay," he answered easily. "I've got my sailboat docked down there."

She shook her honey-toned head firmly. "No way. We're working this morning, Ryan. I didn't drive all the way to La Jolla in rush-hour traffic just to go out and play."

He shook his own chestnut head, his tongue clucking an obvious censure. "Brandy, Brandy. . .how could I get five books out a year if all I did was play? Of course we're going to work."

"On a boat?" she demanded, arching a delicate brow.

"On a boat," he confirmed. "I've got a battery pack for my portable computer. We can enjoy the day and return here tonight, our floppy disk filled with brilliant prose."

He took her hand, leading her across the floor in much the same manner as he had that day at her house. And, as she had the first time, Brandy dug in her heels.

"I can't write on a boat," she protested.

"Of course you can."

"Ryan, I don't want to go out on your boat with you."

"Don't be a spoilsport. Besides, it's my turn to pick where we work. And I pick the *Duskfire*."

"What if I get seasick?" she asked with a mutinous scowl, nevertheless following him out to the car.

"You won't," he answered with certainty.

Brandy slammed her car door before Ryan could shut it for her, inadvertently catching his fingers. He smothered an angry oath, rubbing them gingerly, as if testing for broken bones.

"I'm sorry," she said as he settled himself into the driver's seat.

"Forget it," he muttered, flexing his fingers once again before turning the key in the ignition. "I'm not about to allow your propensity for accidents to ruin our terrific day."

"Speaking of that, if you think I'm such a jinx, how do you know I won't end up sinking the boat? Or throwing up all over it and ruining the wonderful day you've got planned?" Brandy's gaze was half challenging, half admiring. "You're awfully sure of yourself."

Ryan's eyes sparkled with good-natured amusement as he reached out and tousled her hair. "You've got that wrong, sweetheart. I'm sure of you. I just know those gorgeous gams are going to prove to be the best-looking pair of sea legs in San Diego Harbor."

He grinned, his devilish expression backing up a declaration that could have only been mouthed by Johnny Steele. Then, shifting the car into gear, he tore down the curving driveway.

7

BRANDY UNCURLED her white-knuckled fingers from her lap as Ryan pulled the Porsche into a parking space at the marina.

"How in the world do you drive like that without being arrested on a daily basis?"

He grinned. "I have friends on the force."

Brandy stared at him. "That's terrible."

Ryan appeared honestly puzzled. "Would you prefer I spend all my money on speeding tickets?"

"I'd prefer you didn't drive so damn fast."

He studied her for a long, unnervingly silent moment. "That's funny," he offered in a thoughtful tone. "Most women like fast cars. At least that's been my experience."

"I don't."

Ryan was genuinely perplexed. "Why don't you?"

Brandy met his searching gaze with one of total confusion. Why, indeed, should she care how the man drove? Because she was scared to death he was going to kill himself on that curving roadway some day, she admitted silently.

"Perhaps it's because it reminds me of Johnny Steele," she suggested instead in a whisper.

"Perhaps." He stared directly into her eyes. "Or perhaps it's something else altogether."

Ryan looked for a moment as if he was going to say more, but she was given a reprieve as he decided against it. Instead he gave her a warm, inviting smile.

"Ready to test the waters?"

Brandy had already tested them and found them way over her head. "Ready as I'll ever be, captain, sir," she responded with good humor, vowing not to give Ryan any further signals about her feelings. The best way to keep from drowning in this relationship was by keeping things light. And she was going to do that if it killed her.

Boats of all sizes bobbed on the glassy waters of Glorietta Bay, the number of slips demonstrating San Diego's inseparable bond with the sea. Brandy knew all the statistics, having grown up in this birthplace of the Golden State. She knew the spectacular waterfront area was home port for the Eleventh Naval District, housed the world's largest tuna fleet and contained thousands of pleasure crafts. She also knew the harbor had been rated one of the ten finest in the world and that the ocean, in some mysterious and beautiful way, formed a part of every San Diegan's life.

Yet her life had never included any personal experience with sailing, and her eyes drank in the beautiful boats as they rested like strings of pearls on blue satin.

Ryan stopped before a boat that even Brandy's inexperienced eye recognized as a sloop. Approximately twenty-eight feet long, it was large enough to be impressive, but certainly not the most extravagant craft in the marina. It possessed sleek, graceful lines, the dark blue hull seeming to reflect the brilliant water. The deck gleamed with a varnished sheen, and she was relieved she was wearing rubber-soled shoes. It would be a crime to mar such painstakingly achieved perfection.

"Like her?"

She met Ryan's curiously shuttered eyes. "She's beautiful, Ryan, honestly. I know absolutely nothing about boats, but even I'm intelligent enough to be impressed."

The look of pleasure brightened his face, giving him a boyishly attractive charm. "She is a beauty, isn't she?" he asked, unable to keep the note of pride from his voice. "And I've got Johnny Steele to thank for her...."

His words drifted off as Brandy's admission sunk in and he eyed her appraisingly. "You really don't know anything about boats? It's incredible that you could grow up in this city and not have one foot on land and the other on sea."

Brandy fought down the irritation at his incredulous tone. "I don't know a thing, Ryan. Except that they're usually named after women. What's the matter, were you afraid of causing dissension among the ranks?"

Ryan didn't answer as he stepped onto the deck of the *Duskfire*, setting down their assorted supplies. He then extended his hand to invite her aboard. The sloop bobbed lightly on the soft swells of the bay, and Brandy wondered how they'd feel underfoot. She was afraid to take his hand, knowing that there could be no impersonal touches between them. But she was even more afraid of slipping and making a fool of herself. *Better the devil you know*, she reasoned, accepting his help.

As she'd suspected, Ryan was in no hurry to release her. He pressed their joined hands against his chest, his left hand lightly on her back.

"You're right. As it turned out, I probably should have named her after a woman."

"Oh." Brandy pretended disinterest.

"Want to know why?"

"Why?" she inquired warily.

He grinned wickedly and Brandy knew she'd asked for it. "She's trim, responds well to a man's touch, and if the wind is favorable, she'll give a fella a helluva ride."

"You're terrible, do you know that, Ryan Sinclair?" Brandy smiled into his eyes, her expression belying her stern words.

"I know. I've always considered it one of my endearing traits."

Brandy shook her head, thinking that modesty certainly wasn't one of Ryan's stronger traits. Yet she knew that were she honestly to begin cataloging them, she'd have herself an impressive list. He was intelligent, good-looking, had an easy sense of humor and liked kids and dogs. She was certain, having watched him with Kevin and all the other Sinclair offspring, that the man would make a terrific father. And probably a great husband. But not for her, she reminded herself. With a shake of her head, she returned to the matter at hand.

"Enough of the small talk, Sinclair. We've got a book to write."

He released her after a quick kiss, snapping to attention. "Aye, aye, Captain Bligh," he said, saluting her briskly. "But you know what they say about all work and no play..."

"They say it pays the bills," she reminded him firmly. "Now, how do we get this tub out to sea?"

Ryan gave her a wounded look that brightened considerably when Brandy tossed him a conciliatory grin before carrying the portable computer and their other supplies into the cabin.

Brandy stowed the things away, finding the sloop surprisingly roomy. The area below deck was utilitarian, but not oppressively cramped. Ryan turned from where he was taking the cover off the furled mainsail as she returned, his eyes sweeping the empty deck.

"Where did you put everything?"

"In the kitchen."

"Galley."

"Sorry." Why was she apologizing? So she'd called the blasted thing by the wrong name. Not having a firm acquaintance with boats was certainly no crime. Except possibly in San Diego, she admitted.

"Hey, it's no big deal. You'll be an old salt before you know it," he assured her with that dazzling grin that weakened her defenses. "Oh, and while we're on jargon, sailors never go to the bathroom."

"That must be very uncomfortable," Brandy remarked with feigned innocence.

He was preparing to cast off, but stopped to grimace at her poor joke. "It's a good thing you write romances and not comedy routines, lady. You'd starve.... It's called the head."

"Stupid name," she muttered, watching as he moved around with a lithe, masculine grace. "Can I help?"

Ryan looked as if she'd just given him the deed to his very own gold mine. "You really want to?"

She did, she realized with some surprise. Ryan obviously loved this beautiful sailboat, and she wanted to share in his pleasure. Brandy was relieved that she wasn't seasick yet, then reminded herself they were still at the dock.

"You'll have to give me instructions. Unless you want this entire experiment to end up in the head."

Ryan looked up at the fluttering white canvas. "I've always wanted a first mate." He grinned happily, taking a line and pulling it tighter as he trimmed the sail. "Here, take hold of this and we'll cleat it to the top of the cabin."

Brandy found that Ryan possessed that special ability to train a person without ever making the individual feel stupid. He remained patient, leading her step by step through the sailing procedures, not overwhelming her with a myriad of nautical terms. Before she knew it, the sloop was skimming over the waters with a speed that resembled flight.

She was stretched out in the cockpit, the sun beaming down on her face, feeling at peace with the world as they raced along the California coastline. Ryan was absorbed with keeping the sails taut with the wind and she felt free to watch him openly, entranced by the sight of his vibrantly male form.

He'd stripped off his shirt. His skin glistened with sparkling crystals of sea salt left behind as the breeze evaporated the wet spray. He was absolutely beautiful, she decided. And she'd never seen anyone look more at home than Ryan did right now, the wind whipping his hair to a tousled confusion, his eyes squinting against the sun as he watched the fluttering sails, his full lips curved into a smile.

They were sailing past Point Loma, the peninsula that protected the bay from the high seas beyond. She'd placed one of her historical novels at the time of Cabrillo's discovery of the West Coast of the United States. It was here, in 1542, that he'd stepped ashore and claimed the land for God and the king of Spain.

"I wish I'd known," she said aloud, thinking how much stronger the book would have been if she'd seen the most dramatic feature of San Diego's harbor from this viewpoint. The sight fueled her imagination, enabling her to feel the awe Juan Cabrillo must have experienced. Brandy could almost see the Spanish galleons as they entered these waters, sails unfurled, crackling in the wind as they were today.

"Known what?"

"That it could be so beautiful. So perfect," she answered honestly.

Ryan only gave her an understanding smile as he began taking the sails down. He waved off her offer to help, handling everything with a deft skill. When they were anchored offshore from the towering white lighthouse, bobbing lightly on the soft swells, he came over to stretch out beside her.

"I'm starving. How about bringing that food up, mate?"

Brandy shot him a mock glare. "I don't know if I'm wild about being relegated to galley slave, Captain Sinclair. After all, I'm supposed to be a full collaborator."

His eyes gleamed with good humor. "That you are, darlin'. But didn't I do all the expert sailing that got us to this glorious spot? The least you can do is feed me so I'll have the strength to work today.... Or, if you'd rather, we can play instead. I'm sure I could muster up strength for that." The smile that took possession of his dark face was definitely suggestive, and Brandy couldn't resist. She reached out, brushing at the crystals sparkling in the soft mat of chest hair.

"I think I've already learned something very basic about sailing."

He covered her hand with his, pressing her palm against his warm, moist skin. "And that is?"

She lowered her honey head, sighing with sheer pleasure as she tasted his salty skin. She could feel his sharp intake of breath as her tongue stroked his chest, and Brandy knew that she was now the one behaving outrageously. But she couldn't make herself stop.

"I think I've discovered why women are crazy about sailors. They taste so good."

Ryan answered with a sound that was half groan, half laugh, as he pushed her gently away. "Besides being about as capricious as a spring storm, Brandy Raines, you've got lousy timing. As much as I want to spend the rest of the morning and all afternoon making mad, passionate love to you, sweetheart, you've already proved that you're a menace.

"If I give into my more basic urges, I know damn well we'll end up capsizing the *Duskfire* and swimming to shore. So I suppose we'd better eat. Then get to work."

He rose to his feet, pulling her up beside him. "Let's hope none of those tourists taking the lighthouse tour have binoculars."

Brandy's curious eyes followed his downward glance to where his body strained against his cutoffs. She experienced a strange surge of feminine satisfaction at the thought that she could provoke such a response. He was right, of course. As often as she had insisted she had no plans to make love to him, her actions had definitely contradicted her words.

It wasn't that she was lying; it was only that her rebellious body seemed to have developed a very strong mind of its own. And the hunger she was experiencing at the moment was definitely not for the pastries they'd picked up on the way to the marina.

Brandy went to bring up breakfast, suddenly welcoming the chance to escape to the galley, where she could take a few deep, calming breaths unobserved by those bright green eyes.

Although breakfast went smoothly, the first sign of an impending storm came as Brandy finished reading Ryan's first chapter.

"Why do you open with Clint's thoughts?"

"Simple. It's his story."

"It's *their* story," she argued. "I think you should open with Blair in New York, preparing to come back to California."

"Bullshit."

She arched a delicate brow challengingly. "Excuse me?"

He tilted his dark head to the same angle, his green eyes locked to hers. "If you missed it, I can repeat it louder."

Brandy lifted her shoulders in an uncaring shrug. "You can shout it at the top of your lungs, for all I care, Ryan. Just as long as you don't put it into the dialogue. Clint wouldn't use such a vile term."

"It's not vile, it's earthy. And he damn well would. This is a guy who pulled himself up by his bootstraps, sweetheart. Not one of those namby-pamby lords you're always scribbling about."

Scribbling? Brandy fought down the surge of rage his arrogant tone instilled.

"Well, then," she said, smiling with saccharine sweetness, "I suppose then, that horseshit is a more appropriate term. Considering what shape those boots must be in."

He shot her an equally false smile. "Cute, Brandy, real cute. Now, can we just accept it's a stronger beginning opening with Clint's hangover after the funeral?"

Brandy stared out to sea, mentally comparing the two openings. Ryan's was unattractive and gritty. As disreputable as the condition of the hero himself. But compelling, she conceded.

"All right," she agreed reluctantly. "But does he have to drink that whisky before he even brushes his teeth?"

A muscle twitched at the corner of Ryan's mouth. "Have you ever had a hangover, Brandy?"

"No," she admitted, wondering why she should be even moderately ashamed of the fact that she'd never allowed her self-discipline to slip enough to overindulge in anything. Everything about her existence had been kept under tight control—her work, her play and her love life. Until now. Until Ryan.

"Look, honey, this is a guy who just buried his closest friend. Jason Langley's dead and only Clearwater Hills Farm remains. Something he's spent the major portion of his life building and now even that's in jeopardy because the old man's granddaughter will probably put everything up for auction. The poor bastard's life is falling down around his ears. What do you expect him to drink? Hot cocoa with marshmallows?"

Brandy chose not to be offended by the last remark. "All right," she said, sighing. "But the part when Blair enters the room to confront Clint for the first time has to be changed."

He yanked away the paper she held in her hand. "Damn it, Brandy. You can't call it a collaboration when all you do is change everything I write."

Brandy retrieved the sheet, ignoring the ripping sound as a corner remained clutched in his long fingers.

"'Blair's moves painted X-rated pictures in Clint's mind as she walked toward him, her voluptuous hips waving a happy hello.'

"For heaven's sake, Ryan, you make her sound like a stripper."

"She's an extremely desirable woman," he argued. "That reveals Clint's thoughts on the matter."

"No wonder you're having trouble with your heroine. This is an intelligent, sophisticated woman."

"'A dame's a dame,'" he muttered an old line from *The Killing Hour*. "She's no different from any other woman I've put in my books."

Brandy had two alternatives. The first and most attractive was to pick up that battery-operated computer and hit Ryan over his dense, chauvinistic head. The second was to attempt logic. Taking a deep, calming breath, she reluctantly opted for the more difficult choice.

"Ryan, I'll reluctantly admit women like Trixie seem to work very well for Johnny Steele. But we're talking about an entirely different hero. Clint Hollister is every bit as macho as Johnny, but he also has the ability to care very deeply for the things that are important to him—the farm, Jason and Blair."

His jaw jutted forward, but she could see the softening of his emerald eyes. "So?"

"So," she ventured delicately, choosing her words with inordinate care, "do you honestly believe Clint could fall in love with anyone whose 'hips waved a happy hello'? Your hero's a great deal like you, Ryan. Could you fall in love with that woman you're trying to force on him?"

Ryan felt a quickening in his thighs as he met her soft gaze. No, he couldn't. Because he knew exactly what type of woman he could fall in love with. The type who was sitting across from him. Attractive, bright, exciting and as stubborn as a damn trail mule. But right, he acknowledged. So, so right. His subconscious had been trying to tell him that all along, as the heroine had insisted on taking on the characteristics of Brandy Raines.

"You could be right," he muttered.

Brandy's eyes widened. Never in her wildest hopes had she expected such an easy acquiescence. "I'll tell you what," she suggested. "You've got two scenes with Blair in this chapter. Why don't I work on those while you continue on?"

"We have only one PC," Ryan pointed out.

Brandy reached into the duffel bag at her feet and pulled out a long yellow legal pad. "I can work without one."

His eyes danced with merriment and Brandy knew that intense moment had passed. "I forgot. All you historical romance ladies write with a feather, don't you?"

There was no malice in his tone, and Brandy returned his teasing gaze with one of her own. "I'm a renegade," she answered in a stage whisper, as if fearful someone would find her out.

Ryan arched an inquisitive brow as she dug farther into the blue nylon bag, extracting a ballpoint pen with a flourish.

"Absolute heresy," he said, laughing. "But don't worry, sweetheart, your secret is safe with me."

He turned his attention to the small square screen as Brandy read his pages once again. Then her pen began to move across the paper with a speed that would put the fastest typist to shame.

"By Jove, I think you've got her."

Ryan looked up from the sheets of paper, admiration written all over his face. Brandy nodded her thanks, watching him silently. She had a good idea just where Ryan was going to rebel, and he didn't prove her wrong.

"I think you're wrong deleting Clint's thoughts here," he complained, tapping a long, tanned finger against the note pad.

"They were bound to jar the reader, Ryan, shoved into the dialogue like that."

"They were not shoved." His square jaw jutted forward. Brandy sighed.

"Ryan, I'm trying to be on my best behavior, but you're going to force me to tell you that sentence stinks."

"It's your heavy-handed editing that stinks, lady. How in the hell is the reader supposed to know that Clint resents the fact that Blair has taken the fast track to fame and fortune and won't want the responsibility of 424 acres of serene pastures and meadows situated in San Diego county?"

Brandy got up to stand behind Ryan, reading the deleted section over his shoulder. "'Blair McKenzie might be skinnier than his usual choice in a female, but there wasn't an ounce of flesh that wasn't prime. Clint had to remind himself that this dame with the fantastic pelvic structure would screw up his life without turning a perfectly coiffed hair.' This is pure Johnny Steele, Ryan. It'll never work in *Risky Pleasure*."

He looked up at her, his eyes hidden by dark glasses. "I want Clint's thoughts in there, Brandy. Or else the guy will look like a poor slob who can't stand up to a bossy woman."

She had the feeling those thoughts were more Ryan's than Clint's at the moment and said so, which only brought forth a muffled oath in reply. There followed a long, heavy silence as they both stared out to sea. A number of lively dolphins frolicked a few hundred yards from the anchored boat but failed to create a smile on either hard-set face.

"You want to show Clint isn't a pushover, right?" Brandy finally offered into the swirling, stubborn silence.

"Right." It was more a grunt than an answer, but she pressed ahead, anyway.

"How about dialogue?"

Ryan's skepticism was expressed on his face as he turned toward her.

Brandy's mind went into overdrive, trying for a compromise statement. "Why do you have Blair insisting on changes around the farm her first day there?"

"Simple. She's a bossy broad." Even through the dark lenses Brandy could see Ryan's gaze was definitely accusing. "Like most women," he tacked on, in case she'd missed his point.

Brandy had gotten it all right, loud and clear. "I don't believe that was her motive."

An arched brow above the frame of the sunglasses failed to give credence to her argument, but served as some encouragement. Or provocation—she couldn't decide which.

"She wants to prove she knows her way around a horse farm despite the fact that Clint thinks she's nothing but an inane, bubble-headed model," Brandy diagnosed.

"So?" The monosyllable was as close to an admission as she was going to get.

"So, if you want to show Clint Hollister isn't going to be any pushover, have him hit her where she's vulnerable.... Have him tell her right off the bat that he's not going to take her seriously."

Brandy held her breath, watching as Ryan gazed out across the vast expanse of blue waters. His fingers drummed on the yellow pad of paper, his lips pursed thoughtfully as he was profiled against the sun. Suddenly he reached over, took the pen from her hand and scribbled a few lines into the margin. His tanned features relaxed as he sat back with sheer satisfaction, handing her his new version.

"'Look, lady, I'm one of the few trainers on the circuit who doesn't have an ulcer, and I don't intend to get one by having to listen to inane remarks from a woman whose only claim to fame is that she fills a bikini admirably....'"

Brandy rewarded Ryan with a captivating, dimpled smile. "By Jove, I think *he's* got it," she echoed his early words.

Ryan offered his hand. "Shake, partner?" he asked, a conciliatory ring to his deep tone.

Brandy took the hand in hers, emitting a surprised yelp as he pulled her down easily onto his lap.

He yanked off his camouflaging sunglasses, revealing green eyes lit with a menacing mischief. His hands tangled in her hair, letting it drift through his fingers like sifting sands.

"Actually I much prefer kissing and making up to a cold, impersonal handshake."

"How are we going to keep this relationship on a professional basis if we end up like this every time we disagree?"

Ryan tucked a stray length of hair behind her ear. "We could agree not to disagree," he suggested helpfully, his lips moving to caress her earlobe and the point of her jaw.

Brandy felt a little quiver of delight, her body betraying her rapidly spinning senses. "Do you think that's possible?"

"No. I think arguments are inevitable." Ryan's speech was slurred by desire as his lips explored her throat, nibbling at the sensitive cord of her neck.

"Just as inevitable as the fact that we're going to make love before we get to the epilogue," he whispered persuasively, his hungry mouth seeking hers.

Brandy could taste the sun on his lips as Ryan kissed her with a thoroughness that had a crazy effect on her equilibrium. She clung to his shoulders, her mouth opening to the velvet coaxing of his lips. A warmth invaded her body, which had nothing to do with the afternoon sun beating down upon them, and it was only his self-confident words that returned her to sanity.

Unwilling quite yet to give up the exquisite warmth of his body, she lowered her forehead to the hard line of his shoulder, not daring to allow her distressed gaze to meet those beautiful green eyes. While every ounce of common sense Brandy possessed told her that their relationship was becoming far too intimate, her body was still crying out for release. She struggled against the dual sensations.

"Damn. I did it again, didn't I?" he murmured against her hair. His palms stroked ineffectual, calming circles on her back.

"Did what?" she whispered, closing her eyes as she concentrated on gathering up the scattered bits of her self-restraint.

"Reminded you of Johnny Steele. Enough to turn you off."

She shook her head against his shoulder, then slowly lifted her troubled gaze to his. "No. You didn't remind me of anyone except Ryan Sinclair. And no, you certainly didn't turn me off."

Ryan's puzzled gaze searched her face, taking in the love-softened amber eyes that proved her claim. Brandy Raines wanted him as badly as he wanted her. He knew it. So what was wrong now?

"Then why the glum expression?" he asked, his fingers cupping her chin to hold her gaze to his.

"Because I can't handle it," she answered honestly.

Ryan immediately misunderstood. "Are you worried about getting pregnant? We can take care of that, Brandy." He gave her a rueful little grin. "Unfortunately, not at the moment, but since we've already determined it'd be asking for trouble to make love to you on anything that could capsize, we'll just have to wait until we get back home."

How easily he said those words, Brandy considered. *Love. Home.* Two little words that summed up all she'd yearned for her entire life. And they came so trippingly off his tongue.

"It's not that, Ryan. Not at all."

It was his turn to look disconcerted. "Then what the hell is it?" Immediately he regretted his tone as a shadow passed over her tawny irises.

"I'm a writer, Ryan, not a circus performer. If you want a juggler, call Ringling Brothers."

"For a writer, you're damn unintelligible. What the hell does that mean?"

She jumped up, risking capsizing the *Duskfire* as she glared down at him. "Would you mind not cussing so damn much?"

Taking in her stricken expression , Ryan decided not to point out she wasn't doing too badly in that department herself.

"Sorry," he mumbled. "Would you mind trying to explain what's bothering you?"

"I can't juggle a working relationship and a personal one with you. It's as simple as that. I realize I haven't been a model of consistency where you're concerned, but I promise to do better from now on."

Ryan felt like a little boy who'd just been told there was no Santa Claus. "You sound positive about that."

Brandy knew she'd never felt more miserable in her life as she sat back down on the lustrous deck, her knees drawn up against her chest as if for protection. "I am."

He decided he'd never seen anyone so beautiful. Or at this moment, quite as vulnerable as Brandy Raines. "I'd never do anything to hurt you, Brandy. You've got to believe that."

Brandy's troubled gaze drank in his tanned, handsome features. She'd never known anyone so handsome. So nice. And she'd never allowed herself to trust anyone the way she knew she was going to trust Ryan Sinclair.

"I do," she whispered.

"I'm glad," he murmured.

His emerald eyes held her golden ones in a jeweled moment that seemed to last forever. Ryan knew his heart had stopped beating. Brandy was holding her breath.

Fortunately for them both, the raucous sounds of a sea gull shattered the evocative moment as the bird dived, snatching up a leftover doughnut from their breakfast. Both parties to the oddly intimate moment laughed with relief, returning to their work for the remainder of the afternoon.

8

BRANDY GLANCED up sometime later, amazed to see the sun nearly at the horizon. Had they worked that long? Lost in thought, she'd absently eaten the sandwich Ryan had provided as she'd allowed her imagination free rein with the strong-willed characters. She was not surprised that she lost track of time while writing; that was a common occurrence. No, what was amazing was that she'd been able to put aside all those tumultuous feelings Ryan triggered within her and work alongside him.

And work well, she decided, reading the day's production. Ryan's battery allowed six hours on the computer, and sometime during the afternoon he'd switched to the yellow legal pad, as well.

"All in all, I'd say we've accomplished a lot." Ryan rubbed the back of his neck in a weary gesture as he lowered himself to sit beside her.

"And it's good, too," Brandy confirmed. "Despite the fact that I write with a trowel."

Ryan had the grace to redden at the accusation he'd flung at her during a heated discussion of her narrative voice.

They'd stood toe to toe and Brandy had flicked her hair over her shoulder in an angry gesture, her amber eyes flashing sparks.

"Are you accusing me of overwriting?"

"I'm accusing you of laying on the damn metaphors too thick."

"Too thick?" Brandy's resultant shriek scattered a flock of sea gulls.

"With a trowel," he'd snapped, taking his pen and making bold, deleting slashes through three long paragraphs of internal monologue.

Brandy had stared at him for a long, furious moment. The nerve of the man! Her mind spun with a thousand possible retorts. Before she could destroy Ryan with a few of the worst, he marched to the other end of the sloop. That had been their last conversation of the day. Until now.

"I'm sorry about that," he muttered. "I could have been more tactful."

"You could have," she agreed. "I still think you were wrong."

"And I still think I'm right. So what do you suggest we do about it?" The question was one extended sigh of frustration.

"Leave it in and let an editor decide," she suggested.

Ryan held out his hand. "Let me read it again," he requested with patient resignation.

Brandy felt as if she was handing her firstborn child over to the Gypsies as the paper changed possession. She watched him silently, eyeing the skepticism on his face as he skimmed the lines. When he lifted his gaze to hers, he still didn't look convinced.

"Why is it you feel free to slash at my stuff, but if I dare to make any suggestions, you behave as if I'm defacing a shrine." His green eyes were gently censorious. "These aren't exactly the Dead Sea scrolls, Brandy."

He had a point. In fact, if Maggie or her editor had suggested she prune her prose in those paragraphs, she would have seriously considered the matter. It was the fact that the suggestion had come from Ryan, in the form of an arrogant demand, that had set her off.

"I'll think about it," she mumbled.

As if he read her thoughts, there was a relaxing of Ryan's features. Attractive lines fanned out from the corners of his eyes as a beaming smile split his face.

"You do that, sweetheart," he said, his merry tone indicating that he expected total victory in this latest battle of wills.

Brandy couldn't work up any irritation at him. The day had been, with the exception of those few flare-ups, the most delightful she'd ever spent. She reluctantly dragged her eyes from his warm gaze, moving them out to sea, just in time to view the sun deepening from a yellow globe to a molten ball of fire.

Suddenly, before she could catch her breath, it plunged into the panorama of blue Pacific, turning the water to beaten gold. The water was reflected in the billowy clouds overhead, their entire world bathed in a brilliant radiance. The surf turned to gold as the frothy breakers broke on sand that sparkled like a million diamonds.

"Oh, Ryan." Brandy breathed a sigh of pure enchantment, thrilled with the kaleidoscope of colors that turned the sea to a jeweled wonder.

"Wait...it gets even better."

Brandy certainly didn't know how. The gilded waters smoothed glassily outward as far as the eye could see, like a shimmering sheet of gold as the fish flashed silver in the sunlight. Then it happened. As if a giant torch had touched down on the water, the entire sea turned to a flaming, crimson glow. She could almost imagine sparks dancing on the wavelets lapping against the sleek hull as the boat rode at anchor.

"Duskfire," he murmured. "It's my favorite time of day. God, I could see it a million times and never tire of the sight."

The husky timbre of his voice echoed the rumbling surf, and Brandy felt as if she were floating sensuously out of her depth. Her topaz eyes blinked her confusion, struggling to focus on the man standing a few inches away. Her eyes were wide, and softly confused as they searched his face.

She wanted Ryan to make love to her, yet she knew that once he did, their relationship would be irrevocably altered. And quite honestly, she was not prepared to deal with those feelings while her head was spinning in this fashion. It was all happening so fast. Too fast. She needed time to be alone. To think everything through.

Ryan's palm ran down her wind-tousled honey hair, resting on the back of her neck as he held her to a long, silent appraisal. His eyes smoldered with unsatiated passion.

"Brandy—" Ryan began, then stopped as his expression softened. He gave her a crooked grin. "I think it's time we went home," he suggested softly.

Brandy nodded. "I think you're right."

This time Brandy didn't offer to help, something that Ryan was exceedingly grateful for. His self-restraint was at a premium, and he didn't know how long he could hold off if she got anywhere near him.

Brandy managed to spend most of the trip back in the cabin, packing up the day's supplies. She took her time, unwilling to be alone with Ryan on deck. She was relieved that he seemed to share her feelings and didn't press for her company.

When his hands spanned her waist, lifting her to the dock, a sudden surge of heat sparked through her like a jolt of unwelcome lightning. The warmth remained as he laced their fingers together, walking her slowly to the car.

The silence swirled about them, a breathing, living thing as they returned to Ryan's cliffside home. Neither Brandy nor Ryan seemed willing to make any attempt at conversation, no topic seemed safe at this point. In fact, Brandy considered, casting a surreptitious glance at his profile, even sitting alone in the intimate interior of this sports car was not the most prudent of situations.

She could not rid her mind of the taste of his lips on hers, the tang of the salt sparking her senses while his kiss gave birth to quicksilver in her veins. The warm, masculine scent of his skin still gave off the evocative aroma of summer sunshine, and she longed to press her lips against that triangle of dark flesh at the base of his throat.

She could still feel the touch of his broad hands on hers, turning her legs to water as he caressed her with an expertise that might have been Johnny Steele's, but a tenderness that was Ryan Sinclair's alone.

Ryan was aware of Brandy's furtive examination, and it took all his concentration to keep his mind on maneuvering the car up the curving roadway. He allowed himself the idle fantasy of pulling the Porsche over to the side of the road and making love to her then and there. Anything to dispel the sexual tension ricocheting like bullets about the interior of the car. He allowed himself a brief, crooked grin, imagining the hazards involved in making love in so close a space, with that gearshift between them. Besides that, with his luck, they'd get caught by one of the guys from the precinct house. And wouldn't that be just dandy?

Brandy viewed the slight curving of Ryan's lips, wondering what he was so happy about. Could it be the work they'd gotten done today? Could it be the fact that the weather had been perfect, the sea calm, the entire afternoon an absolute delight? Could it possibly be thoughts of her company causing that quirk of a smile?

"Well, I suppose you should be getting home."

Ryan stared out the windshield as the sports car idled in the driveway. Brandy noticed that it whined with impatience at sitting still, reminding her of the barely leashed energy of its owner.

"I suppose I should," she echoed, not making a move.

"I think we got a lot of good work done today." Ryan's voice was strangely impersonal.

Brandy attempted to duplicate his nonchalant tone. "I think we did."

Ryan cut the ignition. Then, as if to fill the resultant silence, he began tapping his fingers on the steering wheel. "Other than those few disagreements, I'd say this collaboration is working out pretty well."

"Very well."

"I thought about it today. I was unfair to hold you to that schedule. We'll switch off places every day, with me doing my share of the driving."

"That's not necessary, Ryan," Brandy protested.

"I want to."

"Oh. All right, then."

A heavy silence settled around them.

"Well, I—"

"Ryan, I—"

They both stopped, looking at each other for the first time as they'd spoken at once.

"Ladies first," he offered. *Say you'll stay.*

"It wasn't important. What were you saying?" *Ask me to stay.*

"You'd better be going," he repeated with a definite lack of enthusiasm.

Brandy stifled her slight sigh, opening the car door. The interior suddenly flooded with light, revealing every wish each participant to the intimate moment was experiencing.

"Good night," she whispered.

Ryan returned to gazing out the windshield, his fingers curved tightly around the steering wheel. "Good night, Brandy."

Driving away from Ryan Sinclair at that moment was the hardest thing she'd ever done. But there was no future for them. She'd made the decision to avoid all emotional entanglements years ago and had stuck to her youthful vow with bulldoglike tenacity. But, she reminded herself honestly, it had never been this hard; never had she been so tempted as she was now.

Ryan watched the taillights of her car disappear into the fog, damning himself for not taking control of that situation. His mind charged into overdrive, trying to determine where he'd gone wrong.

Brandy was as affected by those strange, magnetic forces pulling on them as he was. A natural-born instinct, honed to perfection during his years on the police force, assured him of that. So what in the hell was wrong?

With the tenacity of Johnny Steele when setting out to solve a particularly sticky crime, Ryan sat alone in the Porsche, untangling the sweet mystery of Brandy Raines. After a long, silent time, he went into the house, for the first time really noticing how empty it was.

A long, cold shower did little to lessen his desire for Brandy, and as Ryan sat in the dark, watching the moon-gilded surf crash against the sand, he attempted to sort out his feelings. He wanted her; what man wouldn't? But there was more going on here than simply physical at-

traction. Giving up on sleep, Ryan nursed a single tall
Scotch all night, unable to get Brandy Raines from his
mind.

OVER THE NEXT FEW DAYS, Brandy and Ryan fell into a
comfortable working pattern, discovering that they
worked well together. They spent the mornings writing
new pages, taking a break for lunch before editing the
previous day's pages during the afternoon.

If they were working in Julian, they'd spread a cloth
under a tree in the apple orchard behind Brandy's house,
eating the meal she had prepared before his arrival. On
Ryan's days, they ate out on his terrace, enjoying the sun
and the daily special from the deli down the beach.

"You enjoy your work, don't you?" he asked one day
after lunch as Brandy packed up her wicker picnic
basket.

She gave him a surprised glance. "Of course I do. Don't
you?"

He shrugged. "I love having *written* something. It's the
actual writing that I hate. It's like sweating bullets. Or
blood." He eyed her appreciatively. "You, on the other
hand, seem to thrive on it."

Brandy smiled, rocking back on her heels as she considered his words. "I used to," she admitted, before realizing she'd come uncomfortably close to telling Ryan
something she'd never told another living soul. "Want an
apple?" she offered with feigned cheeriness, tossing one
toward him.

Ryan caught it absently, without removing his gaze
from her face. "Thanks. You know, I'd like to hear that
story."

"What story?" she asked casually, polishing an apple
of her own on her jeans.

"The one you almost slipped and told me before you remembered I'm the enemy," he answered patiently, biting into the apple.

Brandy sighed. "You're not the enemy, Ryan," she objected softly.

"But I'm obviously not much of a friend, either," he protested. "Hell, Brandy, I told you my life story the first day I met you."

Brandy stared across the fields, watching the grass wave in the gentle breeze. "It's not that important," she said finally. "When I was young, I never knew from one day to the next where I'd be living. Who I'd be living with. So I created this family, and every night before I went to sleep, I'd write about them in my diary. After a while, they became more real to me than some of the people I lived with."

Ryan's look was unnervingly gentle. "I can understand that."

Her hands trembled as she twisted the stem on the Red Delicious apple. "After I was on my own, I still wrote stories about my family, but I started trying my hand at other things. Pretty soon I was spending all my free time either writing or reading."

"Romances?"

"Romances, mysteries, science fiction, classics, anything I could get my hands on." A soft smile of remembrance curved Brandy's lips. "I was supporting myself as a waitress in a restaurant near the University of San Diego campus while I went to night school," she revealed.

"Every morning this sweet old man would come in and order two apple Danishes and coffee. Day in and day out, the same thing. We got to talking and I learned he was an English professor at the college. When he discovered I had never read *Pamela*, he just about keeled over."

Brandy laughed as she recalled the day that had changed her life. "The very next morning he brought me a copy, telling me that no one could possibly hope to write a novel without reading the one that started it all. For the next five years the man opened up an entire new world to me. Even after I got a job in an office across town, he made it a point to stop by every day."

Ryan realized how much the old man must have meant to her. Brandy Raines did not let anyone get that close. "Does he still teach at USD?"

A slight cloud darkened her eyes. "He died."

"I'm sorry."

She managed a faint, sad little smile. "Two months before my first book was bought."

Ryan reached out and squeezed her hand. "He knows, Brandy."

She suddenly remembered Suzanne's death coming coincidentally right before Ryan's first sale and realized it was important for him to believe that fervently issued statement himself.

Brandy nodded. "I've always believed that, too," she agreed. Then, extracting her hand, she rose from the blanket, handing Ryan the basket to carry. "Come on," she ordered lightly, "we've left a murderer stalking Clint and Blair. Don't you think it's about time we did something about rescuing them?"

Ryan groaned, muttering about creative sacrifice as they walked, hand in hand, back to the house.

"I've got a confession to make," he said later that afternoon, looking up from the rough draft in front of him.

"A confession?" she inquired absently, making a few notations in the margin.

"Promise you won't kick me out of here and refuse to collaborate on another word?" His solemn tone gained her attention.

Putting the pencil down, Brandy eyed him appraisingly. "Is it that bad?"

He began to pace the floor, his hands jammed into the back pockets of his jeans. "I don't know," he admitted finally. "I suppose it depends on how understanding you are."

Brand put her elbows on the desk, linking her fingers together. Resting her chin on them, she met his worried gaze. "Try me," she invited.

"I've never read *Pamela*, either." He gave Brandy a devastatingly boyish grin, ducking as her pencil flew by his head.

As the book began to take shape, Brandy couldn't help noticing that Clint and Blair's relationship was running parallel to hers and Ryan's. The initial antagonism seemed to have burned out, and as Clint began to accept Blair's presence at Clearwater Hills Farm, Ryan argued less often about Brandy's suggestions. On the other hand, Blair openly welcomed Clint's advice concerning Risky Pleasure, her beloved filly, while Brandy marveled over Ryan's talent for plot twists.

The only problem was the matter of Clint and Blair's love life. The romantic scenes were growing more and more heated, and working on those scenes inevitably left an unmistakable sexual tension lingering in the air. She felt it, and from the way Ryan's eyes darkened as he looked at her lately, Brandy knew Ryan was no less affected. What on earth was going to happen when the day came they could no longer put off writing the lovemaking scene?

Ryan had been giving the subject of the relationship some thought himself during the long, lonely evenings at home. His house, which had once seemed to be an idyllic ocean retreat, now only reminded him of how alone he really was. How lonely. The huge, empty rooms seemed far less barren when Brandy was in them. As did his life.

He still wanted to make love to her, and from the way her tawny eyes softened as she looked at him lately, Ryan knew Brandy shared his desire. Yet although he couldn't define the source, a feeling continued to emerge that whatever was happening between him and Brandy Raines was undeniably special. He sensed they were slowly, inexorably becoming entangled in something far more than a casual affair.

He found his mind constantly wandering to her; during the day, when he was writing Clint's thoughts and feelings about Blair, Ryan realized that the words he was putting on paper reflected his own feelings toward Brandy. At night, as he roamed the empty house or walked along the beach, she was all he could think about and when he'd finally give up on untangling his confusing thoughts, she filled his dreams. She was his dreams.

On the anniversary of their second week of working together, Ryan stood on the beach below the cliffs, his hands jammed into his back pockets as he stared thoughtfully out to sea. But instead of the moon-gilded waters of the Pacific Ocean, he was seeing Brandy's face. The dull roar of the surf echoed about him, but all Ryan could hear was Brandy's soft voice. And as he breathed deeply, it was not the tang of salt air filling his nostrils, but the enticing scent of her warm, fragrant skin.

He had never known a woman whom he could see so clearly when he was alone, whose presence filled some indescribable void deep inside him. Brandy was admittedly a challenge and Ryan had always thrived on challenge. But it was more. So much more.

Then the truth suddenly burst upon him with all the clarity of a crystal mountain stream. He loved her. She'd become the single most important thing in his life and with his characteristic decisiveness, Ryan knew he could not wait until morning to share this wonderful, blinding knowledge with Brandy.

He took the steps up the cliff two at a time, mindless of his knee. Forgetting the hour, he jumped into the Porsche and tore down the hill, headed toward Julian.

It crossed Ryan's mind, as he drove into the hill country, that while the idea of loving Brandy came as a welcome revelation, she might not view it that way at first. During their two weeks of working together he'd come to realize that she was extremely cautious in her personal relationships. If he wanted to play this smart, he'd break it to her gently, allowing her time to get used to the idea.

Although he knew better than to try to push Brandy into anything, as he pulled the Porsche up in front of her house, Ryan's excitement overcame his sense of caution.

"Brandy, open up!" Ryan called out, pounding enthusiastically on her door. "I've got to talk to you."

Yanked from a restless sleep, Brandy jumped from her bed, flung open her front door and stared in disbelief at the man illuminated in the spreading amber glow of her porchlight.

"Ryan, can't you just ring the bell like anyone else? You'll waken the entire neighborhood." Sure enough, as she glanced next door, a light appeared in Mrs. Simpson's house.

He gave her that dazzling grin, reminding her that she was wearing her retainer. Damn.

"Sorry. I just got everything all figured out, and I wanted to come tell you I've solved our problem."

Brandy clamped her mouth shut, talking through pursed lips. She was not about to let this man with the Pepsodent smile see her dental hardware.

"What problem?" She was still blocking the doorway, not inviting him in.

"The one about when we're going to make love," he said simply.

Had she actually heard the astonished gasp, or had her guilty conscience only imagined it? Julian's cool nights allowed the population to sleep with their windows wide open, and the way Ryan's deep voice was carrying on the perfumed night air, Brandy knew that Mrs. Simpson could not have missed his self-satisfied proclamation. She grabbed his arm, pulling him inside her tiny foyer.

"All right," she said, still through clenched teeth covered with firm lips, "what are you talking about?"

He closed the door behind him with a quick kick, then drew her into his arms, his lips swooping down to cover hers without warning. Brandy closed her mouth, embarrassed that Ryan was very shortly going to discover that she was a thirty-year-old woman who still wore braces. His tongue breached the barriers of her tight lips, running along her teeth, encountering the metal bands.

"You should give a guy some warning." He tilted his head back, his eyes grinning down at her. "That stuff can be damn dangerous. When I was fifteen, Cindy James and I locked braces, and it took the fire department two hours to disengage us."

"Liar."

The gold devils danced in his green eyes. "You're right," he agreed unrepentantly.

"I thought so."

"It was our parents. And it only took fifteen minutes. But it sure as hell seemed like two hours. I'll tell you, it was six months before I worked up the nerve to kiss another girl."

His engaging grin was impossible to refuse. Brandy offered a slight, tentative one of her own. "I feel so foolish. No one knows I wear this ugly thing."

He ran his palm down her arm, his fingers entwining with hers as he took her hand, leading her into her comfortable parlor.

"You should've seen the miles of railroad tracks I wore when I was a kid." Again the vivid grin appeared. "We Sinclairs all inherited big, strong teeth. The only problem was, every one came in crooked."

"That's the point," she argued, sitting down on the couch, not complaining as he joined her, his hand still clasping hers. "You were a kid. I'm thirty years old, Ryan."

His bright eyes made a long, slow appraisal of her body. She was wearing a thigh-length nightshirt, tailored in a man's button-down style. Her long legs were curled under her, and despite the lack of ruffles or feminine attire, Ryan had never seen anyone more enticing.

"And you wear your advanced years exceedingly well, sweetheart." He gave her a friendly leer.

"Please don't tease me."

He put his arm around her shoulder, his hand rubbing comfortingly on her upper arm. "Hey, honey, so what if the state of California didn't see fit to straighten those gorgeous teeth? I think it's great that you're able to do it now. It doesn't make you any less attractive, you know."

She met his warm gaze with a level one of her own. "Oh, come on, Ryan. I know what I look like."

He arched a dark brow, inviting her evaluation.

"Ridiculous. Like some overaged adolescent. A thirty-year-old waif," she muttered, turning her head away.

Ryan cupped his long fingers about her chin, returning her face to his. Brandy was surprised to see the tense expression darkening his handsome features.

"Don't you ever put yourself down around me, Brandy Raines. You're a warm, intelligent, attractive woman and I won't let you say a word against the woman I love."

She stared at him.

"That's right, love," he muttered, releasing her momentarily to rake a hand through his hair. "And this wasn't at all the way I was going to tell you. But as usual, you caught me off guard."

"You can't love me," she objected weakly.

"Why not? Even with your propensity for accidents, you're not exactly unlovable, sweetheart. Besides, you're getting better. You haven't bruised or wounded me for at least three, maybe four days.... I want you, Brandy. And I love you."

"Don't say that," she pleaded in a whisper, feeling drawn by the inexplicable tugging on her senses that this man could create with a mere look, the slightest touch.

His fingers traced a trail of sparks from her temple, down her cheek, along the curve of her jaw. Brandy melted into the cushions.

"Why does my loving you make you so unhappy?"

"Because it can't work, Ryan," she tried to explain. "There's no future for us."

"Of course there is. A future filled with love and kids." He grinned. "Do you like dogs? I'm of the school that believes every boy should have a puppy."

"I can't have that, Ryan," Brandy answered firmly, secure in a decision she'd made years ago.

"Are you allergic?" he asked with friendly interest.

Damn the man. He was so blissfully satisfied with his pipedream he wasn't paying any attention.

"Not the dog," she rasped. "That life right out of 'Father Knows Best' you're describing." Brandy wanted to look away, but the firm fingers still held her chin, and his green eyes refused to release her wary gaze.

"Why not? You've already got a man who loves you. As for a family, except for crooked teeth, I'd say we'd make some damn good-looking kids. You're absolutely gorgeous, and I've never been accused of being Quasimodo."

"You're perfect and you know it," she argued. "Just like you know every damn gene that went into you to make you that way."

He muttered an oath that was so amazingly colorful she was surprised she hadn't read it in *The Uninvited Corpse*. Her writer's mind scribbled it on a mental blackboard. Ryan rubbed a weary hand over his face.

"Are you telling me that you've decided never to get married or have kids because you don't know who your parents were?" Ryan's deep voice didn't hold the incredulous tone she'd expected. Instead it was low and resigned.

Brandy had to admit it sounded a little ridiculous, stated aloud like that. But she stuck to her guns. "That's right."

"It really bothers you that much?"

She nodded.

"Then why haven't you tried to find them?"

"I did, a long time ago. I gave up on the idea."

"Why?"

"All the records are sealed, Ryan." There was one additional reason Brandy failed to reveal. In all honesty, she'd never been absolutely certain she wanted to find her natural parents. After a life filled with rejection, she hadn't wanted to set herself up for one that could prove more painful than any she'd already managed to survive.

Ryan took both her hands in his, his thumbs massaging light circles on her skin. His expression was solemn, his eyes lit, not with desire, but determination.

"If I help you locate your parents, Brandy, will you consider a deeper relationship?"

Brandy longed to tell him she'd willingly spend the rest of her life with him. But honesty forced her to acknowledge that even if Ryan could find her natural parents, she couldn't promise him anything. He was a wonderful man. He had a wonderful family. Every instinct she possessed told her that he'd already had a marvelous wife. How could she, Brandy Raines, abandoned nobody, top that? The answer was that she couldn't.

"I can't promise anything," she said softly.

"I'm only asking you to promise you'll give us a chance, Brandy." His deep voice quavered slightly.

"I promise," she managed to whisper.

Ryan's face lit with enough wattage to brighten the entire valley to daylight. He pulled her to him, squeezing her in a bear hug that had her praying he wouldn't crack her ribs. His fingers laced through her unbound hair, tipping her head back into his hand as he rained a shower of happy kisses over her mouth.

Remembering the metal band across her teeth, Ryan took care to be gentle, not wanting to cause Brandy any pain. Yet, there was nothing tentative in the kiss, either, and as her mouth clung to his, she lost herself in the magic his lips evoked. All too soon, he turned those seductive lips into her hair, his breath fanning a warm breeze in her ear.

"Tomorrow we're going to set out to solve the mystery of Brandy Raines," he murmured.

"Tomorrow we write," she argued.

"That too," he agreed. "But it won't take long to run by the Social Services Agency and take a quick look at your records."

She pulled her head back. "For a cop, you sure don't know a lot about bureaucracy, Ryan Sinclair. They won't let anyone take a look at those records. Quick or not."

He winked a vivid emerald eye. "For a writer, you sure aren't showing a lot of imagination, Brandy Raines. There's more than one way to skin a bureaucrat."

He gave her one more reassuring kiss, a brief, silvery flare that ended all too quickly. Then he stood up, pulling her to her feet. He held her for a moment in the circle of his arms, his hands resting in light possession on the small of her back. Tingles raced up and down her spine as his fingers massaged the delicate bones.

Brandy lifted her arms and put them around his neck, leaning into his body. The low moan that issued from his throat indicated Ryan was finding leaving a difficult chore. His hands moved downward to cup her buttocks and she felt his sudden intake of breath as he discovered she was wearing nothing under the tailored nightshirt.

"You're not making this any easier, babe," he groaned, his palms roaming the smooth bareness of her back and hips as he molded the lower half of her body to his length. "I want to make love to you, Brandy."

"I know." Her eyes were liquid amber, revealing her willingness for exactly that.

Ryan shut his eyes against temptation, and Brandy thought how beautiful his dark lashes looked against the polished mahogany of his skin. "I've got to be the biggest fool ever born on God's green earth, sweetheart, but I'd better leave before it's too late."

Brandy couldn't believe her ears. Ryan had been the one pushing for this from the beginning. Even once he'd stopped his seduction campaign, he'd insisted on intimacy, drawing out those sordid little stories about her past.

As Ryan viewed the confusion washing over Brandy's face, he shook his head, his mouth firming into a tight line. "Since meeting you, I've discovered I'm a selfish bastard, honey. When we go to bed, which we will," he stressed, sounding a bit more like that self-confident rogue, Johnny Steele, "I'm going to be wanting a commitment, Brandy. I don't want to be a one-night stand. Or some research project for your next romance novel."

Her eyes widened as she stared at him. Was it possible? Could he have thought she was only interested in using him as a brief, romantic interlude? In the same way she'd accused him of living out Johnny Steele's masculine fantasies? And what did he mean by commitment?

Unable to consider any of those questions right now, she latched on to the most obvious of his statements. "I'd say, Ryan, if you want to get technical, that I'm the bastard." Her words were scarcely audible as she turned away, but he hadn't missed them.

"Damn it, Brandy, if you bring that up one more time..." Ryan was galvanized into action, his fingers biting into her shoulders as he spun her toward him.

When it appeared she planned to make her escape, he gripped her chin hard so she couldn't twist away.

"Listen to me," he ordered on a low note that was far more threatening than any shout might have been. Brandy wondered momentarily if it had been the tone he used to control unruly mobs. She knew it was scaring the hell out of her. The hand on her chin directed her gaze upward into eyes as unyielding as dark green stones.

"Do I have your full attention now?"

She nodded, one last defiant light in her eyes flickering despite her fear.

He jerked his own head in a brief nod, apparently satisfied, seemingly uncaring whether her attention was given willingly or not. Just her luck, Brandy moaned inwardly, to get involved with an ex-cop. A professional storm trooper. She liked her independence; she thrived on it, in fact. Now here she was, being forcefully held in place by a man far stronger than she.

As if on cue, Ryan released her, dropping his hands to his sides. Brandy didn't move, nor did her gaze leave his oddly wounded one. He cleared his throat. "I don't want you to put yourself down like that."

His voice vibrated with tightly controlled emotion. "I'm not one to bandy the word around, honey," he said, his eyes warming to a deep sea green. Brandy fought against the sensation she was drowning in the swirling depths. "If I say I love you, you'll have to believe that I mean it...."

Those beautiful dark eyes surveyed her with great gravity and as Ryan raked his fingers through his already tousled hair, Brandy's keen sense of observation noted they were trembling. The air was charged with emotion as they stood inches apart, green eyes not moving from amber. Just when Brandy thought she could take no more of the finely drawn intensity of Ryan's gaze, the Westminster chimes of her grandfather clock sounded deafeningly, shattering the oppressive silence. The remoteness in Ryan's eyes focused, and she was treated to an odd, crooked smile.

"I've got to be going if I'm coming back here first thing in the morning."

"Yes." It was a whisper.

"We've got a lot to do tomorrow."

"Yes." Was that all she could say?

"We'll shoot for a chapter."

"Yes." *Stop that*, her mind screeched.

"Then we'll go into the city and see about tracking down Brandy Raines's family tree."

"Oh, Ryan." The words were expelled on a regretful sigh, but at least they were different.

He placed a long finger over her lips, forestalling her protest. "Trust me," he half crooned, his beautifully inflected voice like a velvet touch.

She nodded, her gaze equally as solemn. "I do, Ryan. I honestly do." Even as she said the words aloud, Brandy's voice displayed her surprise that they were the truth.

That magic smile lit his face, indicating his pleasure. "That's a very good start," he professed, kissing her far too circumspectly on the lips before letting himself out of her house.

"Lock this door."

Brandy moved slowly to follow his instructions, thinking as she did so that she'd never locked a door while living in Julian, and nothing had ever happened. Ryan Sinclair was just one of those people who liked to storm into people's lives and take full charge. What in the world was she doing, even allowing for an instant that they could have any kind of relationship? She'd been on her own all her life and had survived just fine.

But as she fell into a fitful sleep, Brandy couldn't remember ever finding her bed so incredibly lonely.

RYAN ENTERED the room in the dark, moving unerringly to the large bed. He slumped down onto the mattress, staring out at the vast Pacific Ocean outside the glass wall. The moon had gilded the whitecaps a brilliant silver that shattered as they crashed upon the spilled diamonds of the sands. He stared seaward for a long, silent time, then, reaching over, flicked on the bedside lamp.

Blinking against the sudden surge of light, he reached out, picking up the silver-framed portrait. He studied it, wondering if he'd ever been as young as that laughing woman in the picture. Yet he must have been, for he and Suzanne had been born the same year. They'd gone through school together, married right after high-school graduation, as everyone had always known they would, and had spent the next few years loving and laughing. And fighting, he acknowledged. Suzanne had known him far too long to be intimidated when he pulled his tough-cop routine on her. God, how he'd loved her! He'd accepted it so casually; Ryan had never known a day when he hadn't loved this girl next door.

But now, with Brandy it was like being struck by a lightning bolt out of a clear blue sky. He still couldn't get over it. But love her he did. Ryan silently thanked the fates and Maggie O'Neal for sending her to him.

"It's not that I love you less," he murmured, running his fingers over the Plexiglas-covered face. "It's just that I love her now."

Giving the photograph one last fond look, Ryan rose, placing it in the bottom of a bureau drawer, under a pile of ski sweaters. Then, stripping off his clothes with a weary sigh, he collapsed into the bed, falling asleep immediately.

9

THE FOLLOWING MORNING flew by as Brandy edited their previous day's work and Ryan stayed at the computer's keyboard, the rapid movement of his fingers over the keys indicating his mind was once again focused on Clint and Blair's problems, instead of their own. While Brandy was secretly relieved that he hadn't brought up last night's conversation, all too often she found herself looking up from her pages, concentrating instead on that sun-gilded dark head, those long, tanned fingers and lips that tightened periodically in thought.

Ryan Sinclair would be such an easy man to love, she mused. If only... Then she shook her head, disallowing that rogue thought. Love brought too many disappointments. Her life had been going along just fine before she met him, and as long as she refused to allow her heart to rule her head, it would continue smoothly after the book was finished and Ryan returned to La Jolla.

"Done!" The object of all her soul-searching suddenly leaned back in the swivel chair, massaging the back of his neck with a tired but self-satisfied gesture. "Now we'll print up a hard copy, then go downtown."

"Downtown?"

"Now that Blair and Clint are well into their little adventure, tracking down Risky Pleasure, it's our turn to track down your missing parents."

Oh God, he meant it. "Ryan, I've already told you. That trail has a million dead ends."

He regarded her for a long, solemn moment that had her feeling as if she was being examined by a brilliantly green microscope lens. "I promise you, Brandy, we'll find your family."

Still unable to answer, she escaped the gentle, encouraging gaze as she practically ran to start the printer.

"RYAN, BELIEVE ME, there isn't anyone in here who'll give us the time of day."

They were parked outside the San Diego County Social Services building, a place where Brandy had known her fair share of frustrating failures.

"It never hurts to try, honey."

Brandy shook her head, her disappointment showing on her face and in her eyes. In a private, faraway part of her mind, she'd honestly hoped that Ryan, with all his years on the police force, plus his flair for mystery writing, would be able to help her. But all he was doing was following a trail she'd already marked. A cold, useless trail.

"Ryan, watch my lips. It's no use. These people have sworn to take their secrets to the grave."

He grinned. "Maybe we'll get lucky and find someone who's less dedicated to bureaucratic nonsense. Besides, I've got a secret weapon."

She looked at him skeptically. "And that is?"

The smile widened and he winked a gorgeous green eye. "Charm. Wait and see how devastatingly charming I can be when I put my mind to it."

He was out of the car before she could answer, but as she watched him walk around to open her door, Brandy had to admit that if she worked in that huge building and this man walked up to her counter, she'd tell him any-thing he wanted to know. They'd stopped briefly at his house so he could change, and Ryan was now dressed in a slim gray suit that made him appear more authorita-tive than she'd ever seen him.

Charm worked up to a point, they found, as the flus-tered clerk dug obediently through her backdated files, extracting a manila one bearing Brandy's name. They'd worked their way successfully past five preceding em-ployees of the Social Services division and were now in the tiny, cluttered room referred to as "back records." The plaque on the woman's desk read Ms Martin.

Never had Brandy gotten this far in her quest, and now she sucked in her breath as the woman held the file a mere five feet away. This was her past. Her roots. Her family tree.

"Oh, dear." Ms Martin looked up from her perusal of the folder, directing her attention to Ryan.

"What's the problem?" he asked, his voice neutral.

"This was an abandoned-child case."

"That's right."

"Well, we can't release this information."

Brandy's shoulders sagged visibly, and she felt the air leave her lungs in a depressed sigh. They'd come so close.

Ryan appeared unruffled by the woman's declaration. "This is an extraordinary case," he explained. "There's a great deal of money involved."

Both Brandy and the clerk looked at Ryan with re-newed interest. "Money?" Ms Martin asked.

Ryan noddeed. "Money. And I know that when the proper parties are discovered, they will be very grateful to whoever helped me locate them. You see, the late Miss Raines was my client...."

He ignored Brandy's startled gasp at having been so casually declared dead. "She left a vast fortune, even by today's standards, and her dying wish was that the money be passed on to her relatives."

His smile was warm and encouraging, stopping just this side of bribery. "Of course, I've got to find her family before any of the funds can be unfrozen... Then there's the matter of the jewels."

"Jewels?" Brandy could practically see the dollar signs flashing in Ms Martin's gray eyes.

"Jewels," Ryan affirmed. "The young woman seemed to have a thing for collecting precious stones. She could have probably fed the entire populations of half the developing nations on those rocks she's got stored away in bank vaults."

"I'd like to help." The woman shifted the manila folder from hand to hand, obviously caught between an innate sense of duty and the idea of sharing some of Brandy Raines's imaginary wealth.

"I'm sure the beneficiaries would appreciate anything you could do," he coaxed silkily.

"Do you think so?" There was a hopeful note to the woman's voice. Brandy was holding her breath.

"Wouldn't you?" Ryan countered in a deep, reassuring tone.

The clerk had started toward the counter, the file in her hand, looking as if she'd made her decision. Brandy thrust her hands behind her back, squeezing them together until her fingernails left moon-shaped indentations in her skin.

The shrill interruption of the telephone shattered the expectant silence, and Ryan uttered a muffled curse. By the time the woman ended her one-sided conversation, she'd returned to an efficient, unbending official.

"I'll have to get my supervisor's approval before letting you see the records. Rules, you understand."

Ryan smiled. "Of course. I'd never want you to do anything against regulations, Ms Martin."

She stared at him for a moment, obviously unsettled by the sincerity of his tone. It was apparent that the officious Ms Martin was attempting to decide whether or not she'd only imagined his smooth enticements earlier. She put the file down on her desk and disappeared out a side door.

"Ryan, this isn't going to work," Brandy said as soon as they were alone.

"Hush, sweetheart. I don't have time to talk right now."

Ryan cut her off as he put his palms down on the counter and cleared it with the skill of an Olympic high hurdler. Then, in quick strides, he made his way to the desk, picked up the file, and with one deft movement, replaced the papers with some he extracted from his suit pocket. He was back on the proper side of the counter before Brandy could believe what he'd just done.

"Shut your mouth, darlin'," he said softly. "You'll draw flies."

The jarring noise rang in her ears as Brandy slammed her jaws shut. A moment later, Ms Martin returned.

"I'm sorry, you'll have to get a court order before I can release this information."

Ryan feigned a look of resigned disappointment. "That's fair enough," he agreed. Then, his hand firmly resting on Brandy's back, he pushed her out the door, looking backward over his shoulder. "I'll be back," he promised.

The expression on Ms Martin's face, as she refiled the folder, indicated that she certainly hoped so. Money aside, Mr. Ryan Sinclair was a very attractive man.

Brandy was speechless as they made their way through the winding hallways back out to the parking lot. Wher they were settled in the car, she turned on him.

"Ryan Sinclair, you stole those papers!"

He shook his head, clucking his tongue. "Brandy, Brandy, you're not looking at this reasonably."

"Reasonably! Ryan, you just stole documents from a government agency. And I was an accomplice!" Brandy's voice rose high enough to shatter crystal.

Ryan ran a palm down her hair in an attempt to calm her. "Honey, think about it for a moment. Was Ms Martin going to let us read those papers?"

"Of course not. I told you that before we went inside," Brandy reminded him. "Those files are sealed."

"That's exactly the point. Our dutiful Ms Martin is not about to let anyone read those files. So if no one will ever have access to them, then it won't matter that your grocery list is inside that manila cover instead of your life."

Brandy groaned, still not believing this. "We'll go to jail, Ryan...I've never stolen anything in my life. I don't even jaywalk. And now you've made me into a criminal."

He laughed, a deep pleasant sound that affected her with that familiar spark, even through her distress.

"Honey, I guarantee we'll never be caught. Ms Martin has effectively reburied that file, and no one will ever pull it out again."

He had a point. "It's still theft."

"I suppose you could look at it that way."

"Suppose? Ryan, that's the *only* way to look at it! I can't believe you were ever in charge of law and order around this town if your values are that distorted."

She'd gone too far with that one. A thundercloud moved across his face and he glared at her with a look that would have made the ayatollah blink.

"My values are just fine, thank you. That petty theft isn't going to harm anyone, Brandy. And maybe, just maybe, it'll give you your past. So you can get on with your future."

He was only trying to help her, she realized. Although his methods left a lot to be desired, she was honestly thrilled to have the few papers in her possession finally.

"I thought you said I wasn't going to see any more of Johnny Steele," Brandy grumbled.

The smile she got banished the threatening storm. "That wasn't Johnny Steele, sweetheart. That was pure Ryan Sinclair, at his most charming."

He pulled the papers from his jacket and handed them to her. "Here—read these while I make our getaway."

Brandy stared at the sheets of paper, almost afraid to begin. She'd waited so long. It was scary, in a way, suddenly being given your past on five sheets of eight-by-eleven-inch white paper. She read slowly as Ryan drove back to Julian.

"Well?" Ryan pulled the car up behind hers in the driveway.

"Nothing." Brandy's tone was flat. "It doesn't tell me anything that I didn't already know, Ryan. We may as well have left these damn papers back in Ms Martin's sacrosanct filing cabinet."

Ryan held out his hand. "May I see them?"

Brandy handed them over. "They're useless. After all this time..." Her voice drifted off and she turned away, unable to view the tenderness in his gaze.

"There's a lot here, honey." Ryan looked up from the papers.

"Oh, sure. Abandoned baby found in the back seat of a police car thirty years ago. That's a real hot lead. While I've no doubt Johnny Steele could wrap the case right up, we're not going to get anywhere, Ryan."

"Of course we are," he corrected calmly. He turned toward her, taking her hands in his. "Now here's what I want you to do, sweetheart. Go on in, change into something glamorous and expect me on your doorstep at eight o'clock sharp."

"Why?" she asked suspiciously.

"Because we're going out to dinner to celebrate our good luck."

Good luck? The man sure had a funny way of looking at things, she mused. If he wanted to waste his time on a wild-goose chase, far be it for her to stop him. But she, for one, certainly wasn't going to get her hopes up. She told herself that repeatedly all afternoon, and although Ryan's enthusiasm had not waned when he picked her up later that evening, Brandy continued to warn herself not to succumb to his optimistic mood.

"You were awfully quiet tonight," he observed as they stood under the spreading glow of her porchlight. "I don't think you said more than ten words all during dinner."

"I guess I'm a little tired," she murmured.

"You didn't eat anything, either."

"I did, too," she answered, opening the front door. Ryan shook his head, trying to suppress his irritation that she'd left it unlocked again.

"All you did was push your food around on your plate. You reminded me of Kevin whenever Ellen serves liver." Ryan's gaze held both concern and affection as he framed her face with his palms. "I love you, Brandy," he assured her in a deep voice, "and I'd never promise you anything I wasn't firmly convinced I could deliver."

He grinned suddenly, bending to give her a quick, hard peck on the lips. "As good a writer as I am, wait until you see the investigative cop in action. That guy makes even Johnny Steele look inept."

Ryan released her, taking the steps two at a time, avoiding the loose one. "Get some sleep, Brandy," he advised. "Things always look brighter in the morning." He tossed her a kiss before climbing into the Porsche and driving away.

10

RYAN ARRIVED at Brandy's door early the next morning, his jaunty stride an indication that things were looking up. He knew exactly where he wanted his story to go today; better yet, he knew exactly where he wanted his relationship with Brandy to go. The sun was shining, he'd seen what he now was whimsically considering his lucky hawk circling overhead as he drove up the mountain, and damn, he considered, as Brandy opened the door, did she look gorgeous!

"Hi, there," Brandy greeted him with a smile.

"You look good enough to eat." Ryan's brilliant green gaze glittered as it toured her slender body, clad in a striped T-shirt of soft sherbet colors and white jeans.

Brandy felt the warmth color her cheeks. She wasn't used to blushing and wasn't certain she liked the way Ryan could cause the atypical response to compliments. But he stimulated a great deal of other uncharacteristic feelings that she had to admit she loved.

"How about breakfast instead?"

He braced his hands on either side of the doorframe, leaning forward to within inches of her expectant body.

"Do I have a choice?"

"Of course," she murmured on a silvery note.

The golden sunburst in his eyes visibly flared at that one. "Then I know what I'm hungry for." Ryan shut his eyes and moved even closer, his lips headed toward her smiling mouth.

"Waffles or hotcakes, Ryan. Take your pick," she offered, patting his cheek before turning away, headed for the kitchen.

His eyes flew open, his dark lashes abandoning his cheeks. Ryan stared after her a moment, then exploded into a long, hearty laugh.

"Touché," he said as he entered the kitchen. But his actions were anything but abashed as his hand connected with the back of her jeans and squeezed.

"Ryan!" Brandy spun around, the bowl of batter in her hand. A little bit sloshed over the earthenware rim onto the floor.

He lifted his hands in a defensive gesture. "Hey, honey, do me a favor and put that down before I end up dipped and breaded."

Brandy shot him a nonthreatening glare. "I wasn't going to drop it on you."

He grinned. That devastating, magical grin that pulled at all her senses. "I didn't say you were. It's just that you've got to admit that since we met you've been a walking disaster area. I'm about ready to apply for federal relief funds."

"Very funny. Now what does the comedian want for breakfast?"

"How about the cook?" Ryan gave her a pleasant leer.

Brandy leaned back against the counter, thoughtfully tapping a pink-tinged nail against a front tooth that this morning was once again free of metallic restraints.

"How about a bowl of glop right in your lap?"

He sighed. "You're not going to play fair today, are you, Brandy?"

Her amber eyes narrowed. "Play fair?" she asked suspiciously.

Ryan nodded. "Play fair. You meet me at the door looking remarkably like something that should be in a sugar cone and then deny me even one little bitty lick."

She reached behind her, picking up the bowl. "Oh, did you want to lick the spoon?" she asked with exaggerated innocence, her eyes wide and tawny as they laughed at his disconcertion.

"I give up," he grumbled. "All right, make mine waffles. For now."

Brandy succumbed only momentarily to the bright invitation in his emerald eyes. Then, damning the answering blush she felt warming her cheeks, she turned away to make their meal.

"This is really nice." Ryan eyed her across the table, as he finished his third waffle. "I'm not used to being so pampered."

Is that what she was doing? Brandy thought about it a minute and decided truthfully that she was. It was far more normal behavior for her to mix up an instant breakfast in her blender.

"Don't get used to it," she warned lightly.

He looked absolutely wounded. "Are you telling me that you're not going to feed me every morning once we're married?"

Married? Didn't the man ever give up? "We're not getting married, Ryan."

"Of course we are," he replied easily. "And if you aren't into morning domesticity on a regular basis, we'll make do somehow. How do you feel about breakfast in bed?"

Ryan gave her a look she could have poured on one of those waffles that had disappeared from his plate. Brandy jumped up from the table to escape the desirous expression, grabbing his plate and holding it under running water before sticking it in the dishwasher. She busied herself an unnecessarily long time cleaning counters, scrubbing the sink, even arranging the copper canisters by size. Anything to keep from returning to the uncomfortably intimate conversation.

"Uh, Brandy?"

"What?"

She spun around, her voice at least two octaves higher than usual.

Ryan lifted his mug toward her. "May I have some more coffee? It takes at least five cups of caffeine before I can function with any resemblance to a human being in the morning."

She remembered Ryan had claimed to be a night person and had a pretty good idea of how he usually spent those nights. And it certainly wasn't writing.

"Of course." She brought the Pyrex pot from its warming stand.

Ryan ran his hand up the back of her leg, sending sparks in all directions. Brandy jumped with both surprise and that now familiar shock of desire.

"Oh, no!"

It was a warning, but it didn't come soon enough. Ryan kicked his chair over in his attempt to dodge the flow of hot liquid headed in his direction. Brandy could only stare as the coffee made a spreading dark stain over the denim.

"Damn it, Brandy!"

Ryan's fingers flew to the snap at his waist and he stripped off the soaked jeans before she could open her mouth in protest. He was standing there before her, wearing nothing but a blue, button-down shirt and an indecent pair of bikini underwear in scarlet, of all colors.

She gawked, her wide eyes taking in the corded muscles of his thighs, his washboard flat stomach.

The anger slowly left Ryan's reddened face as he acknowledged Brandy's admiration of his body.

"If you wanted me to take my pants off, darlin', you could have just asked." His white teeth flashed in an amused smile.

Brandy bristled like a porcupine at his masculine ego that dared to make such an insinuation. Once again he was Johnny Steele. To the core.

"It was an accident," she shot back. "I slipped on some batter."

His long fingers were splayed on his hips, drawing her eyes to that particular portion of his superb physique. If other men might be embarrassed by the visibly stirring desire straining the soft cotton, Ryan didn't appear to suffer from any such compunction as he stood in that spread-legged stance, appearing enormously pleased with himself.

"I see." His green eyes, when she managed to drag her gaze back up to them, were filled with passion.

"That's the truth," she protested hotly, wishing right now she had a second pot of coffee to pour over this grinning egomaniac's head.

The roguish glint didn't leave his eyes as they fielded glances. Brandy met only amusement in the steady green eyes while she glowered back at him.

She tapped the toe of her running shoe. "Would you mind putting your pants back on? We may dress casually for meals around here, Ryan, but you are definitely overly informal."

"That coffee was hot," he countered, the smile not leaving his lips. Then it broadened. "A couple more seconds and our chances for a big family would've been shot." The boisterous grin extended to emerald eyes that gleamed with good humor.

Brandy knew it was a trap, but she involuntarily followed that bright gaze downward.

Only to look at him brought her pulse to a fever pitch and swept with a sudden weakness, Brandy reached behind her, bracing herself against the edge of the counter. Her legs turned to water, her mind went numb and she was only aware of the shaft of hot fire blazing in her loins. Her amber eyes appeared as if she were drugged, filled as they were with erotic desire.

The glint of laughter in Ryan's eyes disappeared like a sandcastle under high tide, to be replaced by a look of raw hunger. His eyes had grown as dark as jade and seemed to be consuming her as they feasted on her face. Her mouth was suddenly so very dry, undoubtedly from the fires burning within her, she considered, unthinkingly moistening her lips with the tip of her tongue. The unconscious gesture caused Ryan to groan deep in his throat.

"Ryan..." She spoke his name softly, so very softly that Ryan knew that no music had ever sounded so sweet to his ear.

"I'm only a man, Brandy. Only human..." he warned on a note of whispered torment. "So, if you want this to stop, you'd better stop looking at me like that."

Brandy's mouth was soft and tremulous as she gave him a tender smile. "I can't stop looking at you like this, Ryan. Any more than I can stop the sun from crashing into the sea and creating your brilliant duskfire."

Ryan's only response was a sigh of aching pleasure as he eliminated the small space between them, propelling her into intimate contact. He stripped the T-shirt and bra from her in a hurried gesture, his shirt following as he shrugged out of it. Then, crushing her breasts, he pressed her body to his hard male shape.

Infused with a pain that only Ryan could turn to pleasure, Brandy touched him without restraint, her fingers delving below the waistband of his crimson underwear. Her hands seared their warmth to his fiery loins, her openly erotic caresses disintegrating every intention Ryan had of making slow and wonderful love.

His dark head dipped down to her breasts, and Ryan took a rosy tip between his lips, teasing it with his firm white teeth. Those marvelous teeth Brandy considered the most beautiful she'd ever seen closed down with an erotic pleasure, causing her to cry out his name as his mouth created havoc on one swollen breast, while his hand made love to the other.

A surge of passion washed over her, consuming her in hot, churning waves. Brandy ground her hips against his, seeking a release for the dark force rushing through her body.

"God, Brandy, I can't hold back much longer." Ryan's words emerged on a tormented groan against her lips. He'd never known when he'd needed a woman more. Loved a woman with such furious intensity.

"Don't hold back." Her caressing, probing fingers drew a moan of ecstasy as they curled around him. "Please, Ryan, I need you now."

He needed no further invitation as his hands quickly dispensed with the snap at her waistband. The zipper of her white jeans stuck, and Brandy expelled a sigh of relief into his mouth as she heard the material finally rip and give way. Almost as if in a trance, she stepped out of the jeans and bikini panties, which had dropped down her legs, her fingers pushing on Ryan's briefs, sliding them downward.

Ryan's mouth devoured hers with insatiable hunger, his abrasive, flicking tongue evoking a warmth in her thighs. His hand was between them, roving across the soft swell of her abdomen, over the silky delta of her femininity.

Brandy's hair flowed down her back like a golden waterfall as she threw her head back, the scent of her wildflower shampoo mingling with the essence of desire, causing Ryan's head to swim. Her lips parted in a smile of rapture, and her entire body was warmed with a soft pink flush.

"I don't want to wait any longer, Ryan. Please make love to me now," she whispered persuasively.

His hands cupped the firm, rounded curves of her derriere, lifting her up to poise her above him. Then, slowly and deliberately, he lowered her down his body. At the first contact of flesh against flesh, Brandy cried out, not in pain but in anticipation.

"Oh, Ryan," she breathed into the warm, male fragrant skin of his neck. His name on her lips could have been a prayer, it sounded that sweet to him.

Her long, slender legs curved about his lean hips, her arms wrapped around his neck as he moved expertly, filling her with aggressive male strength. For a moment he remained still, letting her body adjust to the feel of him deep within her.

Then, as a quiver of pleasure rippled through her, he began to move, his broad hands guiding her hips, moving her in an age-old rhythm as he drove against the warm center of her passion. Brandy clung to Ryan as if he were a lifeline, her only salvation in the whirlpool of primitive need that threatened to engulf her. Her fingers curved like pink-tipped talons into the hard line of his shoulders, her thighs pressed tightly against him.

She was safely braced between the counter and the tensing rigidity of his body, but as he dragged his mouth from her lips, pulling his head back to engage her own love-filled eyes in a sensual duel, Brandy experienced the feeling of drowning in a stormy green sea. His eyes were dark and wild, his body relentless as he filled her with an elemental strength. The little eddies that spiraled outward from her innermost core were replaced by a hot tide of desire that washed over her, consuming her in churning waves. Brandy clung to Ryan, riding the cresting breakers as the warmth swelled and cascaded, her climax causing a deep tremor that was almost cause for disaster as she jerked backward, momentarily throwing Ryan off balance.

His arms were full of her as he struggled to maintain their heated fusion, refusing to relinquish the warmth of her body quite yet. He pressed her back against the counter, lifting her and lowering her to ride on his hard strength until the resultant explosion racked his body. On unsteady legs, Ryan managed to make his way to a chair, carrying Brandy with him.

They remained that way, for a long, silent time, suspended in sensual fulfillment. The only sounds in the sunlit kitchen were that of Ryan's deep drafts of air and Brandy's own ragged breathing.

"I love you," he murmured finally against her hair.

An involuntary sigh escaped from Brandy's lips, one he took as an argument.

"I'm not just saying that, Brandy, because I feel a responsibility to, after what just happened."

His beautiful eyes were no longer a tempestuous sea, but now resembled deep green pools, the golden flecks looking like warm afternoon sunshine. Unable to meet his gaze any longer, she buried her head in his shoulder.

"Don't do this." Ryan's voice, still husky from their lovemaking held an unmistakable plea.

"Do what?" she said against his warm, moist skin.

"Ruin it by feeling guilty. I love you, Brandy Raines. And there's nothing wrong with showing you how I feel."

She could feel his smile against the top of her head. "Although I can't say that performance demonstrated much expertise or restraint. Next time, I promise I'll love every inch of that gorgeous body."

She flung her head up, causing his teeth to come together with a resounding crack. She'd been going to tell him that there certainly wouldn't be a next time. That this had only been an aberration caused by mutual attraction. Nothing more. She couldn't allow herself to become any more emotionally involved with Ryan Sinclair than she already was.

But all those words vanished from her mind as she stared in mute horror at Ryan's face. His astonished shout of pain stopped in midyelp as he viewed her expression.

"Do I have any teeth left?" he asked weakly, testing gingerly with his fingertips.

"Of course you do," she assured him in a faint voice. "Let me see."

When Ryan opened his mouth with a mock smile, Brandy thought she'd cry. They weren't caps, after all. And now his beautiful smile looked more as if it belonged on a jack-o'-lantern.

"You've chipped your front teeth," she groaned, feeling horribly, incredibly guilty.

Ryan's tone held a kind of weary resignation. "When you spilled that coffee on me, I thought it was today's quota. I guess I was wrong."

Her palm stroked his cheek. "Poor dear. Does it hurt very badly?"

"Like hell," he admitted. "How many nerve endings do you suppose there are in teeth, anyway?"

Brandy slid from his lap, gathering their strewn clothing with hands that only shook slightly.

"I don't know. But, I do know we have to get you to the dentist right away.... Oh, Ryan," she wailed, "I am so very, very sorry."

He rose from the chair in a lithe movement, standing there, running his finger tentatively against what used to be the loveliest teeth she'd ever seen. He appeared unconcerned that he was totally naked. And no wonder, Brandy considered, thinking of the pain he must be in.

Amazingly enough, he flashed her a grin. "That's okay, honey. You didn't do it on purpose. Besides, they were only teeth. I hear it's astonishing what dentists are doing with plastics these days."

The jagged smile and his steadfast good humor only caused Brandy to feel even worse. "But they were such beautiful teeth, Ryan...and...and..." She drew a deep breath, gathering strength to tell him the truth. "And I have a confession to make," she finally got out.

An unbelieving brow climbed his tanned forehead. "Don't tell me you planned that little act of assault and battery?"

She covered her face, unable to have him see the guilt etched onto her features. "No," she admitted. "But I was incredibly jealous of them, Ryan. It just seemed so unfair that a man would have something so beautiful, while I..." Her trembling voice drifted off.

Ryan's deep chuckle astonished her as he pried her fingers from over her eyes. "Well, then, I'm glad it happened. Because you're a tough enough nut to crack, Brandy Raines, without worrying about the jealousy angle."

Again he flashed her that reassuring smile, which only served to make her cry. Giving up, he climbed back into his clothes and agreed to let her do the driving to his dentist in San Diego.

"You know, people are really going to think I've been beating you if you don't turn off the tears," he commented casually as she parked the car in the medical center's parking lot.

"Then stop smiling at me."

Brandy felt guilty enough about the fact that she seemed to be a walking menace to Ryan Sinclair. Her heart broke every time he gave her one of those ridiculous, encouraging, snaggle-toothed grins.

"You want me to scowl instead?"

The resultant glare was so out of character that Brandy had to laugh. He didn't even do it well. There was still that ghost of a smile hovering at the corners of his tight lips.

"Weird lady," he muttered, opening the door and getting out of the car. "Smile at her and she bawls her pretty head off. Snarl and she laughs. What a crazy broad."

He reached out and ruffled her hair with a tanned hand before they entered the dentist's office.

—————————— //11 ——————————

BRANDY TRIED TO KEEP HER MIND on the magazines in the dentist's waiting room, but she might as well have been reading Sanskrit. She couldn't get her mind off whatever was happening to Ryan behind that closed door. Finally, after what seemed an eternity, he emerged, looking a little pale, but in his usual good spirits.

"What do you think?" Ryan asked, bestowing a dazzling grin on Brandy that didn't go unnoticed by three waiting women patients, one receptionist and two young dental assistants. All seven women, Brandy included, stared at the flashing white crescent brightening the handsome teak face.

"You look almost as good as new," she said truthfully. "Are they caps?"

"Temporary ones. It'll be a week, ten days before the permanent ones are ready. Until then I'm only allowed to nibble on soft things."

His sparkling eyes moved over her body, liquid emerald insinuations that caused the dental assistants to giggle. Brandy fought the blush that had only become a habit since meeting Ryan Sinclair.

"Are you ready to go?"

He nodded his sun-kissed head. "All ready to go home and have you administer some tender loving care. I just have a prescription to pick up on the way."

She responded with a nod, refusing to meet the speculative glances of the other women in the waiting room. She knew, were she to ask for volunteers, that each and every one would suddenly develop an intense interest in nursing.

Since Ryan's car was at Brandy's house, she had no choice but to take him home with her after stopping by the pharmacy. The prolonged dental treatment had caused the nerves of his shattered teeth to throb and she'd gotten a paper cup of water from the pharmacist, allowing Ryan to take the prescribed pain pills immediately.

"I think it might be better if we didn't try to get any work done today," she suggested, eyeing his oddly ashen face.

She could tell he was trying to be as macho as Johnny Steele, but the look of gratitude on his face was more like that of a twelve-year-old boy who's just been told that school was unexpectedly canceled for the day.

"Good idea," he agreed instantly.

"So you can go on home and I'll come over to your place tomorrow."

He shook his head. "Uh-uh. Can't do that."

"It's not your fault we won't get any work done today, Ryan. I'm forfeiting my day to work here."

He shook his head again, his words oddly slurred. "Uh-uh. That's not what I mean."

Brandy looked at him suspiciously. "What exactly do you mean?" she inquired stiffly, her hand on the car door handle.

"Here. Read." He shoved the vial of pills toward her.

"'May cause drowsiness. Use care when operating a car or dangerous machinery,'" she read aloud, looking up to see a look of sheer innocence on his darkly tanned features. "Are you telling me...?"

He grinned, a boyishly attractive smile. Brandy noted irrelevantly that the two temporary caps were not quite as white as the rest of his teeth and hoped the permanent ones would be a better match.

"I'm really sleepy," he mumbled, his nodding head and glazed eyes confirming his words. "You wouldn't put me in a car and send me back down these mountains like this, would you?"

"You knew this when you took those damn pills back at the pharmacy, didn't you?"

"Of course I did, Branny...uh, Bandy...uh, darlin'." His eyes kept drifting shut even as his slurred words confirmed her accusation.

Brandy heaved a sigh. Getting out of the car, she helped Ryan into her house. The tiny Victorian dwelling only possessed two bedrooms, one of which was filled with a word processor, printer and walls of bookcases. There was only one bed. Hers.

"This is real hospitable of you, darlin'."

He smiled a dazzling smile as she led him into her frankly feminine room and stopped before the wide, four-poster bed.

"Don't get any ideas," she warned, wagging a threatening finger. "When those pills wear off this afternoon, you're going home."

"Home." He nodded gravely.

"Take off your clothes and I'll wash those pants," she suggested, eyeing the jeans that still bore the dark brown stain of this morning's coffee.

"I'll always take off my clothes for you, pretty Brandy." His fingers moved to the buttons on his shirt. "Are we going to make love again?"

"We most certainly are not," she said curtly, turning away before she could view that hard mahogany chest and be tempted to change her heated vow. After a long silence, she glanced back over her shoulder.

Ryan's tongue was between his lips, making him look like a little boy as he concentrated on the buttons of his shirt. Earlier he'd managed them with a single hand. Now, as he gave the matter full attention, his fingers seemed to have turned into ten thumbs.

"Here," she said. "Let me." She stood in front of him, easily unbuttoning the shirt.

Oh God, how she wanted to touch him. Just for a moment. Just skim her palms over that soft mat of chestnut hair, which looked as though it should feel like steel wool but resembled spun silk instead.

"Thank you, Brandy. Would you like me to undress you now?" he inquired helpfully.

Her hand, which had been on its way to his chest, jerked backward as if burned.

"I certainly do not. I have no intention of coming to bed with you."

He grumbled, his fingers fumbling ineffectually with the snap at his waistband. "Damn. I thought that's why you brought me in here."

"I brought you in here, you dumb oaf, because you're obviously drunk out of your mind on those pain pills. I'm trying to keep you out of trouble."

She yanked the quilt from the bed and folded down the sheets. When she turned back to him, Ryan was giving her an absolutely angelic smile.

"Let's keep out of trouble together," he suggested.

His hands gave up manipulating the suddenly difficult snap and reached out and shaped her shoulders instead, drawing her into a warm embrace. Brandy closed her eyes to the evocative memories being in Ryan's arms evoked. She told her hands to stop pressing against his back even as she warned her lips that they'd be in trouble if they kept sprinkling kisses over the warm moist skin of his shoulder.

She knew she was playing with fire; she knew that in one minute she'd forego every honest intention she had when she brought Ryan into her bedroom. If his breath continued to fan warmly and wonderfully against her neck, she'd make love to him in an instant.

It was the steady beat of his heart against her breast and his soft, even breath that had Brandy drawing back her head, eyeing Ryan curiously. His lush dark lashes were resting on his cheek, his lips parted slightly, soft sighs just this side of snores humming with a steady rhythm.

He was asleep. He was leaning against her, sound asleep, his seduction attempts disappearing under the effects of the narcotic.

"Damn," she muttered, not knowing whether to feel deprived or relieved.

Instead she stepped back, giving him a shove, feeling she should be shouting "Timber" as he fell backward onto the mattress. Other than issuing a slight grunt, there was nothing to indicate Ryan was aware he'd been moved.

"You have been nothing but trouble for me since you showed up outside my door with your damn Johnny

Steele mentality," she muttered, unfastening the snap of the jeans and drawing them down his legs.

"You've kidnapped me, you've talked me into a collaboration that will probably *never* work, you've wormed your way into my life, my bed, and damn it all to hell, Ryan Sinclair, you've made me fall in love with you."

She gave a final yank on the jeans, pulling them from his body, then threw the flower-sprigged sheets over his silent form. She didn't look back as she marched from the room, but if she had, she would have viewed one vivid emerald eye watching her leave. Then, a broad smile of masculine triumph splitting his face, Ryan burrowed into the soft down pillow, allowing himself to ride the drifting tides created by the powerful pain pill.

Brandy continued the story where she and Ryan had left off the day before. She was self-conscious in the beginning, Ryan's accusation that she'd been writing with a trowel still grating. But the lighter style gradually became more natural, and her fingers flew over the keyboard.

From time to time she checked on Ryan, disturbed when he seemed to give no indication of waking. Finally, late in the afternoon, she called the dentist who told her not to worry, that some people responded to the painkiller in that fashion.

"He's been sleeping for five hours, doctor," she said firmly, refusing to allow the man to get back to work until he'd done a better job of convincing her that all was well.

There was nothing to indicate Ryan was in any danger; his color was good, he was snoring blissfully and a smile curved his lips every time she'd tiptoed in to check on him. But damn it, nobody slept like that.

"Ms Raines," the calm, authoritative voice droned in her ear, "I've got Ryan's records right here in front of me. The last time I prescribed that medication was when he had an impacted wisdom tooth extracted..."

There was a slight off-key hum and Brandy could hear him flipping through the charts. "Ah, here it is." The deep chuckle was anything but professional. "What you've got on your hands, Ms Raines," he informed her pleasantly, "is a cheap drunk. The last time Ryan Sinclair took that particular painkiller he was out like a light for twenty-four hours."

"Twenty-four hours?" My God, he couldn't stay here that long. It would mean him maintaining possession of her bed all night.

"Twenty-four hours," the dentist confirmed on a deep, knowing laugh. "If he's still asleep this time tomorrow, give me a call. Otherwise, you should have no problem."

Brandy somehow managed to hang up the phone without slamming down the receiver. No problem? How dared the man so blithely state that opinion. She had an overstuffed couch with two bad springs, a hammock between two elm trees in her backyard and one four-poster bed, which was at this moment occupied by a nearly naked man. No problem?

"Think again, doc," she muttered, going into the bedroom once again to stare at Ryan with renewed intensity, as if she could waken him by telepathy. Giving up, she went back to work.

Hours later she returned to the bedroom, taking a short cotton nightshirt from a bureau drawer. She opted for a padded wicker chair in the corner of the bedroom, telling herself that she was only sleeping in here so she'd be nearby if he awoke in pain and needed something. It certainly wasn't because the sheet had slid down to his waist, the slanting moonlight coming in the window displaying the vivid contrast of her pastel sheets and his darkly tanned chest.

Ryan was lying on his back, one hand flung over his head, and from the smile on his lips, she knew that whatever wild dreams those pills were causing, they must've been dandies. It was the same provocative grin he bestowed on her whenever he was thinking of making love to her.

Stop that, she told her mind as it spun sensual pictures every bit as erotic as those probably marching through Ryan's drugged brain. She pulled her quilt up to her chin, curled her legs under her and settled down to sleep, refusing to spend one more second thinking about the man lying just a few feet away in her bed.

Much, much later, Brandy straightened her legs with a soft moan, stretching her stiff arms above her head. This was ridiculous. She couldn't get any decent sleep in this chair. It was her bed, after all. And Ryan wasn't due to regain consciousness for hours, if what the dentist told her was true. And she was certainly a grown woman capable of saying no. Just because she slept with a man didn't necessarily mean anything had to happen.

"Ryan, move over," she instructed briskly, pushing the tanned legs stretched diagonally across her mattress.

"Umph?"

"Move your legs, you big moose." She lifted them up, swiveling his body, dropping them back to the flowered sheets with a thud.

"Brandy?" His tone was muffled and slurred, but his velvet voice still managed to do something warm and wonderful to her name. "Is that you?"

"It's me," she acknowledged, crawling into bed, clinging to the very far edge of the mattress.

Ryan's eyes still didn't open, but he reached out with unerring accuracy, pulling her to him. Burrowing his head in the soft hollow between her breasts, he settled in like a bear making preparations for the long winter.

"I'm glad you came to bed, Brandy. You feel so nice. Umm. Soft."

Brandy stared down at the dark head resting in the V-neck of her nightshirt. She could just push him over to his side of the queen-size bed. She could yell bloody murder until he woke up enough to trade places with her and sleep on the uncomfortable chair himself. Or she could just stay where she was and savor the forbidden sweetness of having Ryan lying there beside her, his long hairy legs entangled with hers as he held her in his arms.

Making her decision, Brandy pressed a light kiss onto the top of his head and shut her eyes, drifting off to a wonderfully satisfying sleep.

SHE SLAPPED at the annoying tickle several times before finally waking up enough to realize the tantalizing touch was Ryan's.

"I'm sorry I woke you. I just wanted to brush your hair back so I could see your face."

Her hand reached up to still his continued gesture. "Don't."

"Why not?"

"Because I look a mess in the morning, that's why."

Ryan ignored her protest, pushing a long, thick strand of golden honey hair from her cheek. His green eyes moved in a slow, masculine appraisal of her face.

"You look like an angel in the morning," he argued, his knuckles brushing along the cheekbone he'd just uncovered.

The delicate gesture left a trail of sparks on her skin, and Brandy jerked to a sitting position, wrapping her hands around her knees.

"How are you feeling?" she asked.

Ryan groaned. "Like I've got the world's worst hangover. What the hell did we do last night?"

Brandy stared at him, startled by the question. Didn't he remember? He did look honestly awful. Her judicious gaze took in a pewter gray complexion darkened by a black stubble of beard. His eyes were heavy lidded and looked as if even to blink would cause him pain. His brow was furrowed in thoughtful lines, his features a mask of discomfort.

"You don't remember?"

Ryan's eyes made a valiant attempt to come to life as he reached out a palm and ran it up her arm.

"Of course I do," he alleged on a velvety deep note.

Brandy's amber gaze narrowed. "You do?"

"I remember the important stuff."

She lifted a delicate arched brow suspiciously. Didn't the man ever give up? "Such as?"

"Such as the good time we had together in this bed," he replied, his hand tracing the slender line of her collarbone.

"It *was* good, wasn't it?" Brandy gave in to the impulse to spin her little trap and allowed herself a falsely reminiscent smile. Her eyes were liquid amber as they roved over the harshly chiseled features of his pain-etched face.

"The best, babe, the best."

Something in the tone was too much like Johnny Steele and Brandy jumped from the bed to stand with fingers splayed on her hips.

"You overconfident, egotistical masher!"

Ryan responded to her shouted attack by clutching both sides of his head in his hands, moaning as he closed his eyes. Then one brilliant green orb popped open.

"Masher? What outdated dictionary did you pull that one from?"

"Outdated? What do you call that sleazy line? Even the infamous Johnny Steele couldn't get away with that one!"

He sat up, resting his forehead against his bent knees. When he lifted his gaze to hers, she noticed that the usually vivid whites of his eyes were crisscrossed with an angry network of dark red lines.

"Brandy, sweetheart, do you think we could do without so much volume this morning? Someone's pounding away with a jackhammer in my head."

At his honest look of misery, Brandy almost found herself relenting. Almost. But not quite.

"It's absolutely disgusting the way all you think about is sex," she hissed, lowering her voice.

Brandy told herself her softened tone was not in any consideration for Ryan, but because the window was open and she wasn't about to give Mrs. Simpson any additional grist for the town's gossip mill.

He looked thoroughly confused. "I don't only think about sex. But I thought we were talking about last night."

"We were. And the only thing that happened last night, hotshot, is that you snored like a bull moose and hogged all the covers."

Ryan raked definitely unsteady fingers through his hair. "Then why in the hell do I feel this way?" He ran his tongue over his teeth. His green eyes narrowed as he tried to remember.

Brandy couldn't resist the look of despair and returned to sit on the edge of the mattress. "It was the pain pills the dentist gave you," she said softly, jogging his memory.

Ryan pursed his lips thoughtfully, then a glimmer of comprehension widened his eyes. Ignoring his pain, he sprang from the bed, practically flying past her as he made his way to the bathroom. A low, muffled moan revealed he'd seen the temporary caps and remembered.

"They're only temporary, Ryan," Brandy soothed as he returned and slumped down into the chair she'd abandoned in the middle of the night. "I'm sure when you get your permanent ones, no one will ever be able to tell."

He returned her comforting expression with a bleak stare.

Brandy tried again. "If it's any consolation, I thought they were caps, anyway."

He looked at her with tortured eyes. "Brandy, those were my front teeth...." There was a note of grievance in his voice. "Hell, if I'd wanted replacements I'd have taken a hammer to them and gone out and bought new ones. But I liked those teeth just fine. The way they were."

Brandy stiffened in self-defense. "I'm sorry, Ryan. It was an accident. I certainly didn't do it on purpose." She gave him an earnest look. "I'll be glad to pay for the caps."

Ryan drew a long breath and released it wearily. "That's okay, honey. I'm overreacting."

A silence settled over them, and Brandy watched ruefully as Ryan continued to run his tongue over the plastic caps. They had been the most beautiful teeth she'd ever seen, she admitted secretly. In some odd way, she felt like a murderer.

"There's an extra toothbrush in the medicine cabinet, Ryan. And if you don't mind shaving with a pink razor, you're welcome to use mine. And I'll fix you some juice and coffee to get you started. Then we'll figure out what you're up to eating for breakfast."

He rose slowly, a glimmer of light returning to his eyes as they made a slow appraisal of the expanse of tanned leg extending from her thigh-length nightshirt.

"Is that the same pink razor you use on those legs?"

Brandy nodded, waiting for the traditional masculine complaint about sharing razors with women.

"I like that idea" was all he said, but she couldn't help noticing his eyes looked a little brighter as he walked past her to the bathroom.

"How's the head?" Brandy handed Ryan a glass of freshly squeezed grapefruit juice as he entered the kitchen a few minutes later.

"Not good." He grimaced. "I should've remembered about those damn pills. I don't know which feels worse, my head or my teeth."

Brandy placed the first of what she knew would be many cups of coffee in front of him, her heart softening as she saw him slumped at the table, head resting in his palms.

"I don't suppose it would be a good idea for you to take any more of those pain pills."

"You're right. It'd be a lousy idea." His voice was muffled as it came from behind his hands.

"I've got some aspirin. We could try that," she suggested helpfully.

Ryan lifted his head, his red-veined eyes thanking her. "That'd be a start...although I know what would probably take my mind off the pain."

He managed to give her a crooked grin, which she knew was intended to be seductive, but instead it broke her heart. She turned away, unable to view those alien caps.

"Brandy?"

Ryan was behind her, his hands on her shoulders, the puzzlement obvious in his voice.

She turned to face him, anguish etched on her features. "Oh, Ryan...I'm s-so s-sorry... I've ru-ruined your b-beautiful smile!" It was a wail, one born of a strange self-pitying guilt, and Ryan drew her into his arms.

"Hey, it was an accident, remember?" His tone held an obvious concern for her feelings.

She lifted misty eyes to his face, loving everything about it. She traced the outward fanning lines at the corners of his green eyes, then massaged lightly at the deep vertical cleft etched between his brows at her distress. Her fingertip ran down his slightly pug nose to his lips.

He caught her wrist, holding her hand still while he pressed kisses on her fingertips, one by one. Then he ruffled her morning-tousled hair and returned to his chair.

Brandy knew he'd been wounded by her accusation that all he thought about was sex. She realized that Ryan Sinclair's feelings went far deeper than that. Just as she realized he was willing to ignore the electricity that had been arcing between them only a moment ago in order to prove himself nothing like Johnny Steele.

She was not accustomed to anyone caring so about her feelings and was more terrified than ever of allowing herself to love this marvelous man. He was too good for her; one of these days he'd figure that out for himself. She couldn't bear the thought of Ryan's deserting her, but knew it was inevitable. That idea was suddenly so depressing that she pushed it away.

"Would you like your coffee warmed up?" she offered in what she hoped to be a fairly steady voice.

Ryan shot her a look of absolute dread. "I've got an idea. Why don't you go get dressed? And I'll get my own coffee."

She took no offense at his words. Instead, she leaned back against the counter, folding her arms across her chest.

"You don't trust me." There was a hint of a smile quirking at the corners of her lips.

Ryan shook his head. "Honey, I think you're gorgeous. I think you're intelligent. I am also willing to admit that you're a very good writer..."

"But," she offered, helping him out.

"But you're an accident just waiting to happen. And to tell you the truth, my poor old body can't handle any more battering. I'm not getting any younger, you know."

Her eyes took a quick inventory of his lean, lithe body. Maybe he wasn't getting any younger, but he was looking better to her by the moment.

When she finally dragged her eyes back to his face, she was met with a teasing, provocative gaze. He was right, she decided on an inner groan. The atmosphere in this room was getting far too explosive. She'd take a shower and get dressed, then return with a more professional attitude. *A cold shower*, she added to herself as she passed the rumpled bed on the way to the bathroom.

"This stuff is damn good." Ryan looked up as she entered the room twenty minutes later.

"Really?" She'd thought so while writing it, but had secretly expected complaints when it came time for Ryan to read the chapter she'd completed yesterday.

"Really." His green eyes returned to the hard copy she'd run off the printer before going to bed. "Why did you stop when you did? It looked as if you were on a run."

She poured herself a cup of coffee, sitting down across the table from him.

"I was. But to tell you the truth, I didn't want to go into the horsenapping scene. Because I didn't have the faintest idea how to go about it."

He lifted his cup to his lips and Brandy's eyes followed, watching the movement of his tanned expanse of throat as he swallowed. *Dear God, look at me*, she thought with honest agony. *I'm even in love with the way the man drinks coffee.*

His eyes were thoughtful as they observed her over the rim of the cup. There was an obvious lack of desire in them, and Brandy realized he'd shifted into his work mode.

"I think that Clint should be the one in charge of the search for Risky Pleasure. After all, we've been letting Blair run the ranch."

"Something she's been doing quite nicely," Brandy felt the need to point out.

He nodded, grinning. "Agreed. But, Ms women's libber, if Clint is allowed to track down the filly, it'll show he's of real value to her...more than just a good-looking stud." His voice had an odd quality that Brandy didn't recognize.

"That's why I left that scene for you," she reminded him calmly. "If you feel you're up to it, that is. Perhaps we should just take you home and start in again tomorrow."

"Trying to get rid of me, Brandy?"

"Of course not, it's just that—"

He reached across the table, covering her hand with his on the tablecloth. "I'll be on my best behavior from now on. You won't see one more hint of Johnny Steele from Ryan Sinclair. I promise."

There was a solemn intensity to his words that rendered Brandy speechless. She could only nod her acquiescence.

12

THEY WORKED throughout the day, Ryan demonstrating that whatever pain he was in, it didn't affect his writing ability. Brandy decided such self-discipline must have come from those days he'd been forced to write after a full shift as a San Diego patrolman. He turned down her offer of lunch, only accepting more aspirin every few hours. Finally, as the sun began to set, he pushed away from the desk.

"I'm starving," he announced. "Is there any place around this rustic burg that serves soup?"

"Do you feel like going out?"

"Not really," he admitted, running his tongue over the temporary caps."

"Then why don't you stay here?" she asked casually.

"Is this an invitation?" His eyes were smiling, even clouded slightly with the pain he'd been successfully hiding all afternoon.

"Only for soup. We're eating at home."

"At home?" He arched an inquisitive brow.

"Here," she amended, thinking how odd it was that it seemed perfectly natural to have Ryan in her house. She hated the idea of sending him back to that magnificent seaside dwelling. She'd be lonely, she realized.

From the time Brandy had reached legal majority, she'd lived alone and enjoyed it. But suddenly, since Ryan's arrival in her life, alone had turned to lonely. She didn't know what she was going to do when the book was finished and there was no longer any reason to see him.

"That's a great idea," he agreed. "I want to make a few phone calls first. If I can be of assistance, just holler."

He left the room, opting for the phone in the room she used as a den. Brandy felt a stab of disappointment when he failed to give her the light kiss she was expecting. Then she realized he had every intention of keeping his word. She'd be seeing no more Johnny Steele seduction attempts. If she wanted any more lovemaking from Ryan Sinclair, she'd have to initiate it. Brandy didn't know if that made her feel better or not.

"That was delicious." He'd finished four bowls of the robust Italian onion soup, his appetite echoing his compliments.

"Thank you. Would you like some dessert? I've got some ice cream I can top with Kahlua."

He shook his head regretfully. "I'd love it, but I've got to go. I'm late for an appointment."

"Oh."

Damn. Why hadn't it occurred to her that Ryan was used to a nightlife that did not include hanging around homey kitchens?

"I didn't say a date," he said softly, viewing the distress wash over her features. "I said an appointment."

Brandy rose from the table, taking the two empty bowls to the sink. "Really, Ryan, I couldn't care less what you do on your own time. Our only agreement is to collaborate on this book. When it's done, we'll both go our separate ways."

Her words sounded false, even to her own ears, but Brandy still couldn't believe these wonderful days could continue forever. There was something wrong with her, something she'd never been able to discern, even during long hours of soul-searching or staring at her reflection in the mirror. Yet others must see her intrinsic flaw as easily as if she wore it on her breast like a scarlet letter because no one had ever wanted her.

Her dreary thoughts returned to one foster parent who'd spent his weekends deep-sea fishing, only bringing home the best of his catch. Keepers, he'd called them. Brandy Raines had never been a keeper.

"Goddamn it, woman, would you quit acting like an idiot?"

Ryan's voice sounded like the roar of a wounded lion as his fist hit the table, causing the water in the glasses to rise in wild waves.

"For your information, I'm going out to talk to a reporter friend of mine. To see what we can dig up on a certain thirty-year-old news story."

"Oh." She felt like an absolute fool.

"Oh," he mimicked. Then he looked at her with renewed interest. "Were you by any chance jealous?"

She rinsed the dishes, refusing to meet the teasing gaze she could feel directed at her back.

"Not in the least," she lied.

"You're the most impossible female I've ever met," Ryan said in exasperation.

"And I'm sure you've met a bunch," she muttered.

"Brandy." It was a low growl, a primal warning she foolishly chose to ignore.

"You're going to be late for your appointment," she reminded him.

There was a moment of dangerous silence and although she didn't dare face him, she could feel his frustrated fury. The short hairs rose on the back of her neck and her arms broke out in goose bumps. The sound of his chair scraping on the floor was deafening as he rose from the table. She held her breath, waiting to feel his hands on her. But the slamming of the front screen door and the roar of the Porsche's engine indicated that Ryan Sinclair had finally had enough.

FOR TWO DAYS she heard nothing from him. Then, just when she'd decided the man had dropped off the face of the earth, he reappeared, not offering any explanations for his absence. Nor did Brandy have the nerve to ask for any.

Ryan effectively set the mood, reading the pages she'd written, making one small suggestion, then laying out the final two chapters. Blair and Clint's love life was progressing far better than theirs, Brandy considered miserably.

There was no longer anything personal in their relationship. They worked well together, spending the necessary hours writing, but then they'd separate until the next morning. There'd been not a hint of Johnny Steele in Ryan's attitude, but neither had there been any of his steadfast good humor. The man projected no emotion whatsoever.

He allowed Brandy the lion's share of writing the love scenes, only interrupting to curtly interject Clint's thoughts from time to time. Unfortunately he wasn't utilizing any of those short, pithy phrases so characteristic of his detective series, so she couldn't even fight with him.

The lack of response was driving Brandy crazy. After two weeks of his correctly polite behavior, she stopped eating; her refrigerator resembled Ryan's—empty except for a few basics. The scant amount of sleep she did get each night was filled with dreams of him, in happier times. Before she'd chased him away with her inability to open up.

Now Ryan had effectively built a stone wall around himself, and Brandy didn't have the faintest idea how to breach it. She was too inexperienced in human relationships, and was proving a total washout at love. Her time ran out as the book came to an end.

Blair and Clint discovered the pilfered filly in Tijuana, hidden under a coat of shoe polish, of all things. Fortunately, a heavy rainfall had proved the horsenappers' downfall.

"I've found a guy who knows your mother."

The casual pronouncement, made at the end of the day as Ryan prepared to leave, caught Brandy off guard. Her fingers froze on her glass of Coke, and it fell to the table, the liquid spreading across the polished surface to drip onto Ryan's Levi's cords.

"I thought my luck was going along too well. It's been more than two weeks since you attacked me," he said resignedly, only moving to save the stack of papers that were the result of the final day's production.

Brandy watched the steady drip of dark liquid with an unwilling fascination. "You haven't gotten close enough for me to do any damage," she said, her eyes on his lap as it received the major portion of her soft drink.

"That's the way you wanted it," he reminded her.

"That's what I said I wanted," she agreed softly. The unstated message hung in the air between them, and she knew Ryan read it.

"Do you have a paper towel?" he asked finally.

Brandy almost knocked the chair over in her haste, returning with an entire roll. Tearing off a long strip, she began dabbing furiously at his wet pants.

"I think this is one of the best accidents we've had so far, don't you?"

His voice was melted honey as it smoothed over her. Brandy's eyes flew to his face momentarily, surprised to hear the suddenly intimate tone. Under her hand, she felt a stirring that indicated nothing had changed. Nothing at all.

He wanted her. And she wanted him. But had anything really changed between them? Brandy wanted to open up to Ryan. She wanted to accept the love he was offering. But she couldn't. Dear God, she couldn't shatter that last shield she'd erected about herself. It had always served as her protection, keeping people out so she couldn't be hurt. But now it had become a self-enforced prison she could not escape from.

Her hand flew from the frankly masculine desire, and she shoved the paper towels at him.

"Here, Ryan—surely you can handle a little spilled Coke."

She turned her attention to mopping up the table.

"We'll have to stop at my house on the way so I can change."

She turned to look at him. He hadn't moved. "Where are we going?"

"The Driftwood.... It's a bar."

She shook her head. "I don't go to bars, Ryan."

"You'll go to this one, Brandy."

There it was—that masculine self-assurance. She hadn't heard it for weeks.

"That's what you think," she countered.

"I don't think. I know."

"What makes you so damn sure of yourself?"

"Because the police car you were abandoned in was parked behind the Driftwood. The bartender's the guy who's going to tell you who your mother is. Tonight, as a matter of fact."

She couldn't move. Her legs had turned to stone. Salt, she considered. Like Lot's wife. Never look back, wasn't that the moral of the story?

Ryan took the paper towel from her hand, unbending fingers that clutched it like desperate claws.

"Go get ready, Brandy. It's time for the final chapter."

She waited in the car while Ryan changed, needing time alone to gather her tumultuous thoughts. He seemed to understand, not pressing her to come inside. Neither spoke as the gold Porsche tore down the winding road toward the Coast Highway.

"Ryan, is this man still a bartender at the same tavern? After all these years?"

He shook his head. "Nope. A few years ago he deeded title over to his son. Now he just sits around and chews the fat with the regulars. The place has been his home for too many years for him to abandon it with retirement."

"Oh. Is he nice?"

Ryan heard the slight tremor in her voice and knew she was scared stiff. But not as scared as he was. Because if all his work tracking down this lead turned into nothing, he'd be right back where he started. And with the damn book finished, he wasn't certain Brandy would agree to keep seeing him.

"He's nice," Ryan reassured her. "And he sure remembers you. I got the impression you were one of the high points in his life. He named you, by the way."

The tone of Ryan's voice encouraged a smile and she managed a weak one. "He did?"

Ryan was driving through the waterfront district now and stopped at a red light. He turned to look at her, his gaze warming her face like summer sunshine. It had been

so long since she'd received such a tender look from him
that Brandy had to hold her hands together in her lap to
keep from flinging her arms around his neck.

"It was your eyes."

"My eyes."

"He told me that everyone was standing around looking at you kinda helplessly and the woman from Social
Services kept insisting you have a name for her forms.
You were old enough that your eyes had changed from
the normal baby's blue to an amber, which Jake decided
reminded him of the finest imported brandy. Nobody
down at Social Services saw fit to change it. I personally
think the guy did a helluva good job."

His own gaze was locked onto her tawny eyes, deliv-
ering a thousand provocative messages that had nothing to do with this conversation. God, he loved her, Ryan
considered, not for the first time certainly, as he allowed
himself to drown in the deep amber pools.

His heated gaze was making this harder and harder for
Brandy. The light turned green and still Ryan hadn't
taken his attention from her.

"What about my last name?"

He cast a frustrated glance into the rearview mirror as
an impatient driver sounded a horn behind them. Shifting gears, he moved the car through the intersection.

"Guess," he invited as they turned into the parking lot
of a harbor bar.

"I suppose you're going to tell me it was raining that
night."

He took the keys from the ignition, giving her a
friendly, unthreatening smile. "That's it," he confirmed
cheerfully. "But think of it this way, honey, in this town
you could've very likely been called Brandy Sunshine.
I'd say you lucked out on that one."

Lucked out. What a weird way to put it. What was it about Ryan Sinclair that he was able to find the silver lining in every cloud? Was he like this when he'd been a street cop? Could an eternal optimist stay alive out there without having his beliefs shattered? For the first time she understood Johnny Steele. That was the part of Ryan's personality that survived the more unpleasant aspects of life. Johnny Steele had undoubtedly been the man on the street, dealing with the day-to-day aspects of city crime.

As she entered the darkened tavern, Brandy hoped she was in the company of Ryan's alter ego. Her eyes blinked, her pupils widening as they tried to adjust to the dim light. The clientele appeared to have come from the merchant ships docked just outside the door. Strong, tough and overtly curious, the men's eyes were on her as she and Ryan made their way to the end of the bar.

"Hey you really brought her.... I'd know those eyes anywhere." A large man whose ruddy face was topped by an iron-gray crew cut greeted Ryan.

"They're unforgettable," he agreed. "Brandy Raines, you were a little young the last time you met this fellow. Let me introduce you to Jake Foreman."

It was a rather formal introduction for this place, she thought. But this was not a casual occasion. The man held the key she'd been seeking all her life.

She held out her hand. "Mr. Foreman."

Brandy's slender hand was immediately engulfed in one far beefier. "Hell, honey, the name's Jake. I wouldn't know how to answer to any other...." He turned black eyes down the bar. "Hey, don't you old sea dogs have anything else better to do?"

Immediately heads swiveled back to the television mounted on the wall. Brandy was seeing clearly now and knew she'd been an object of curiosity. It was nice of Jake, she decided, to attempt to give her some privacy.

"Come on—we'll go sit in that corner booth where we don't have such an audience," he directed. "Hey, L.J., bring me another." He glanced over at Ryan and Brandy. "What'll you two have?"

"Beer'll be fine," Ryan said. "Draft."

"I'll have a soda water with a twist," Brandy ordered, not needing alcohol to stimulate the already drunken feeling she was experiencing. Her heart was beating triple its natural rhythm as she awaited Jake Foreman's information.

"Make that a boilermaker, a brew and a spritzer for the little lady, L.J." Jake's voice boomed over the country-western music blaring from the jukebox.

As if by mutual consent, the trio remained silent until L.J. had delivered their drinks to the back table.

"L.J.'s my kid," Jake announced as the bartender walked away. "You and he were born the same winter, missy."

"About that." Brandy cupped her fingers around her glass, leaning forward. She wanted to know. Now. There'd been enough small talk.

Ryan's knee nudged hers under the table. "What's the L.J. stand for?" he asked conversationally.

Jake threw back his head, finishing off the shot of bourbon in quick swallows, then allowed himself a broad laugh. His belly shook under the black T-shirt.

"Little Jake."

Even Brandy, impatient as she was, had to allow a slight smile at that one. Little Jake was six foot seven, at least. With a body that would dwarf a tanker.

The older man wiped the beer foam from his mouth with the back of his hand, his laughing gaze moving from his son to Brandy.

"It appears I did a helluva lot better job naming you, Brandy Raines."

"I believe so," she agreed. "Now about that—"

This time, it wasn't so subtle. Ryan's foot came down hard on hers. Brandy stifled the yelp and shot him an angry glare. His expression was noncommittal.

"L.J. was telling me things are a lot quieter these days than when you ran this place," he said to Jake, an obvious invitation in his tone that the man responded to immediately. His beefy red face beamed with pleasure as he began to tell a colorful tale concerning a brawl between some tuna fishermen and a group of bikers.

Three hours later, Brandy had soda water up to her eyes, her lungs were filled with cigarette and cigar smoke, and her head ached from the continuous blaring of the jukebox. But she also had a name. Her mother's name.

"You can use the telephone in my office," Jake suggested. "It'll give you more privacy than the pay phone."

Brandy was suddenly striken by an almost paralyzing fear. After all these years she finally had an opportunity to talk to her mother. Her real mother. So why was she hesitating?

Ryan squeezed her hand reassuringly. "Want some company?" he asked softly.

She nodded, her eyes revealing her appreciation. "I could use a little moral support," she admitted.

Her legs felt like water as she made her way to the small, clutter-filled back room that smelled of Jake's cigar smoke. As she tried to punch in the numbers on the touch-tone telephone, her hand was shaking so badly she misdialed.

"Let me," Ryan offered, taking the slip of paper. A moment later he handed her the receiver.

Brandy listened to the ringing tone, secretly praying no one was home.

"Hello?" a feminine voice answered and Brandy gripped the receiver with renewed strength, wondering at the ability of an ice-cold hand to perspire.

"Hello, Mrs. Baxter? Mrs. Marianne Baxter?"

"That's right."

Brandy shot a desperate glance toward Ryan, who was leaning against the desk. He nodded encouragingly.

"Mrs. Baxter, this is uh, your..." Her voice faded away as her mind scrambled to come up with the correct term. Daughter seemed highly incongruous under the circumstances. "This is Brandy Raines," she said on a rush of breath.

"I've been expecting your call," Marianne Baxter replied in a far steadier voice than Brandy's. "Jake told me he was meeting with you this afternoon."

"Oh."

Of course, Brandy considered, Jake would not have released the information without receiving prior permission from her mother beforehand. For a fleeting moment Brandy wondered at the relationship that had spanned so many years. Could Jake possibly be her father?

She squelched that whimsical thought immediately. The ex-bartender honestly seemed to care about her need to discover her parents. He wouldn't have bothered to help her and then not be fully open with her.

"I saw you on the 'Today Show' once. I didn't know you were my daughter, of course. You're very beautiful," the woman offered into the heavy silence. "But I'm not surprised; you were always a beautiful baby. A good baby, too. Sometimes you slept so soundly I'd pinch you to make you wake up and cry, just so I'd know you were all right."

Brandy wondered why, if she'd been such a terrific baby, her mother had seen fit to abandon her. She tried to ask, but the words wouldn't come. Ryan, sensing her distress, came up behind her, looping his arms about her waist and pulling her back against him. She leaned into his strength, feeling unreasonably safer in his arms.

Marianne Baxter tried again. "I'm afraid I was a very nervous mother. I couldn't quite learn the knack of relaxing. It was all so overwhelming..." Her voice drifted off, too, as if she was suddenly lost in memories that were more than a little painful.

Then she seemed to recover, her tone steadier, stronger. "I've always hated telephones. They're so impersonal. Why don't you come up to Oceanside tomorrow and we'll have this little chat in person?"

Brandy nodded. Realizing the gesture was ineffective over the telephone lines, she said, "I'd love that."

"So would I," Marianne responded on a note of relief. "We've got a lot of catching up to do."

"Thirty years," Brandy said softly, as if perhaps her mother had forgotten her birth date.

"Thirty years," Marianne repeated with an obvious sense of wonder. "Isn't that odd? I know it's actually been that long, but there are times it seems like yesterday."

Brandy didn't know how to answer that, so she didn't try. "Well, I guess I'll see you tomorrow then."

"Fine," Marianne agreed. "Why don't you come by around eleven? We can talk, then have lunch."

"I'll be there," Brandy said instantly. "Tomorrow, at eleven."

"Eleven," Marianne confirmed. "I'm looking forward to meeting you, Brandy."

"Me too," Brandy breathed fervently. "Goodbye, moth—uh, Mrs. Baxter."

"Please call me Marianne; Mrs. Baxter is far too formal under the circumstances, don't you think?"

Well, she hadn't asked to be called *mother*, but Brandy knew any woman would be a little distracted at meeting her grown daughter for the first time. There was bound to be a period of adjustment while they got to know each other. Then she'd have a family—a real family!

"I agree," she answered. "Goodbye, Marianne."

"Goodbye, Brandy."

Her mother broke the connection but Brandy continued to stare at the receiver, trying to convince herself this wasn't merely a fanciful dream. Ryan gently took it from her hand, replacing it on the cradle.

"I'm having lunch with my mother tomorrow," she said, her eyes wide as she looked up at him.

"So I gathered." Ryan hoped Brandy wasn't expecting too much from the meeting, but the glow in her tawny eyes had him worried.

"My mother. After all this time." Her warm gaze met his concerned one. "How can I ever thank you?"

Ryan said a small, desperate prayer that Brandy would feel the same way about all this tomorrow afternoon. He realized that while she had been forced to grow up self-sufficiently, there was a romantic streak running through Brandy Raines a mile wide. Her books were proof enough of that, but from the soft smile on her lips he knew she was romanticizing her relationship with Marianne Baxter. He wanted to save her from any more heartache, but realized reluctantly all he could do was stand by and help pick up the pieces, if necessary.

"We'd better go," he suggested suddenly, forcing those thoughts away. There was always the chance the two women would hit it off from the start, finding in each other something that had been missing from their individual lives.

He put his arm around her shoulders as they left the office. L.J. was behind the bar, Jake was back on his customary stool at the end. Ryan gave him a thumbs-up sign as they walked past, exiting into the deep purple shadows of dusk.

Brandy suddenly realized how late it had gotten. "Why in the world did we spend all that time in there? We could have gotten that information from him in ten seconds," she complained, rubbing her temples with her fingertips. "Boy, if that's how you interrogated suspects, I'm amazed you managed to get any criminals off the San Diego city streets, Ryan."

His right hand moved to the back of her neck, massaging the tense muscles lightly as he drove. "Would you have preferred Johnny Steele just to throw the guy against the wall and threaten to kick out his lung if he didn't spill the beans?"

Brandy sighed, lolling her head to the magic of his fingertips. "No, of course not. But surely there's a middle ground?"

"Jake already told me he wouldn't take any money, honey. All we were doing was paying for information."

"But if he wouldn't take any money..."

"The old guy's been hanging around that joint for years. There's not a customer in the place who hasn't heard those stories a million times. We gave him a new audience for a few hours, Brandy. And he gave you your mother. I'd say that's not such a bad trade."

She slanted a quick, surprised look at Ryan, unable to see his expression in the profile presented in the streetlights.

"You're a very nice man, Ryan Sinclair," she murmured, placing her hand on his thigh.

"I've been telling you that from the beginning," he reminded her blandly. "Now if you want this very nice man to behave himself, I'd suggest you move your hand."

Brandy's fingers traced widening concentric circles on the denim covering his leg.

"Brandy..." His tone offered a low warning.

"I've missed you, Ryan."

"You've seen me every day... Damn it, Brandy!" Ryan's voice cracked as her fingers grazed into forbidden territory.

"I haven't seen Ryan Sinclair. I've been working with an unfeeling robot," she countered. Her fingernails made a scraping sound against the denim as they ran down the inside of his leg.

"That's what you said you wanted," Ryan reminded her through gritted teeth.

"I was wrong. Don't take me back to my place, Ryan. Let me come home with you."

Ryan's body and heart fought with his head as he attempted to choose the most prudent course. He had a good idea why she'd changed her mind and it wasn't very flattering.

He didn't answer, but Brandy knew she'd gotten her wish as he headed the Porsche in the direction of La Jolla instead of the Laguna Mountains. She stopped her seductive gestures, but allowed her palm to remain on his jeans-clad thigh as she accepted his silence.

"DRINK?"

She turned from watching the crashing surf. "No thanks. I've had enough soda water to float a battleship. Speaking of which. . ."

"I'm not going anywhere," he said simply, slumping down onto the sofa.

Brandy gave him a hesitant smile before escaping momentarily to the bathroom. When she returned, Ryan was sitting with his hands dangling between his knees, holding a glass of dark amber liquid. The expression on his face was definitely dour for a man expecting to make love.

"Ryan? If you don't want to any longer, I'm certainly not going to force you." Brandy's voice was soft and trembled slightly as she sat down beside him, her hand on his shoulder.

Ryan shrugged, rising from the couch with a jerky gesture. "Damn it, Brandy. Of course I want to. I always want to. It's all I think about... Making love to you... But why are you doing this? Tonight of all nights?"

Her finger traced random patterns on the blue material of the sofa. "You mean before I see my mother?"

"Honey, are you going to bed with me tonight because you want to pay me back for finding her? Is that what all this is about?"

Brandy's eyes widened with shock. She'd never thought Ryan might consider it that way.

"No, of course not."

"Is it because you're finally willing to admit you love me?"

She couldn't escape the steady jade eyes and although she wanted to admit her feelings to Ryan with all her heart, her lips wouldn't obey her mind. Instead they settled for a middle ground.

"I need you, Ryan. I'm frightened and I need to feel your arms around me." That was true, but there was more, so much more she couldn't tell him.

He closed his eyes in a slow, accepting blink. Then muffling a soft oath, he put his glass down onto a table and crossed the floor, pulling her into his arms.

13

BRANDY WAS UNPREPARED for the hot, furious mouth that covered hers, devouring her lips with savage, carnal intent. Her surprised gasp allowed Ryan's tongue to plunge into the velvet opening, a pillaging, probing conqueror.

His hands moved below her waist, holding her against his body as he demonstrated exactly how difficult it had been to keep his hands off her these past weeks. Ryan dragged his lips away from her mouth, allowing her gulps of lifesaving air as he scorched a trail down her neck, his teeth taking nips of her warm, fragrant skin. Brandy was infused with a liquid warmth that flowed through her veins like molten gold and she clung to him, fitting her soft feminine curves into his hard strength.

Then, as quickly as the assault had started, Ryan's mood changed. His tongue stroked the tormented flesh of her throat, soothing the skin that had been grazed by his new, permanent caps. His touch gentled, skimming her curves with tender hands. As his lips covered hers in a soft kiss of promise, Brandy expelled a blissful sigh into his mouth.

"This time I'm going to prove I'm capable of a little restraint," he murmured, his lips plucking at hers, punctuating his words.

"I never complained about the last time," Brandy whispered, her hands combing through Ryan's sun-brightened chestnut waves.

In actuality, Brandy had been as desperate as Ryan for that tempestuous lovemaking they'd shared. She'd even thought that once she'd consummated the physical aspect of their relationship, she'd be rid of the constant yearning she felt for Ryan Sinclair.

But she'd learned something that morning. She'd learned that she could never get enough of this man. She'd willingly given him her body. But he'd stolen her heart.

Ryan ached to profess his love, but was afraid to take a chance on ruining this sensual mood. Instead he allowed his smoldering emerald eyes to portray his message as he took her hand, silently leading her into the bedroom.

Thank God the photograph's gone. Brandy breathed a silent prayer of thanksgiving as he placed her gently on the bed and stretched out beside her. A fragment of her consciousness realized the importance of that, but she was unable to consider it fully. Instead she focused all her attention on the feelings Ryan was creating with his marvelously skilled hands.

Ryan searched her face, seeking the withdrawal he was used to seeing whenever Brandy's emotions threatened to get the best of her. He wanted this time to be special. He wanted it to linger in her mind for the rest of her life, whatever happened to their relationship. He wanted every man from this day forth to pale by comparison. Since he'd never forget Brandy Raines, he wanted to make damn certain she'd never forget him.

But more than that, he wanted to give her pleasure. His heart soared as she looked up at him, her tawny eyes filled with emotion. For the moment she'd lowered her parapets.

He undid the first button of her blouse with gentle fingers, pressing his lips over the delicate hollow at the base of her throat.

Brandy's fingers curled beside her as her full lips issued a slight moan. As she responded to his swirling tongue, her blood seemed to throb in her veins.

When her inarticulate sounds demonstrated rising impatience, he unfastened the next two buttons, allowing access to the front closure of her bra.

"Beautiful," he murmured. "You're absolutely perfect, Brandy."

Her fingers uncurled from their grip on the spread, reaching out to unbutton his shirt in return, but Ryan caught her hands, kissing each fingertip before pressing his lips into her palm.

"Just lie still, Brandy. This is for you. I want you to relax and enjoy, sweetheart."

His head lowered to allow his tongue to caress her skin with moist strokes, swirling around and around, moving closer and closer to the taut rosy crowns that reached for his touch, like roses opening to the sun.

"But what about you?" she gasped as the tip of his tongue flicked teasingly over a dark nipple.

He lifted his head, his green eyes home to those dancing gold devils, which had been absent for far too long.

"We've got all night," he replied, twirling an imaginary mustache. "Don't worry about me."

Before Brandy could utter a word, Ryan had returned his attention to her breasts, his teeth closing on one ravished nipple with an erotic pleasure. Brandy's hips lifted off the mattress in response, but true to his word, Ryan seemed in no hurry as he treated her other breast to the same sweet, savage torment.

"Ryan...my God."

Brandy's head tossed on the pillow, her hair flowing out like strands of spun gold as her body warmed to a fiery glow. All sense of time and space had been suspended, and she didn't know whether Ryan had been making love to her for an hour or an eternity. All she knew was that she was in danger of exploding with spontaneous combustion.

"That's it, honey. Don't hold anything back."

His mouth covered hers, his tongue brushing across her teeth before seeking the moist dark vault where hers lay hidden. Ryan's tongue teased and coaxed her own, engaging it in an erotic dance for lovers. Brandy's lips closed about it as Ryan began to plunge and retreat, in a silent pantomime of the lovemaking to come.

Brandy's hands flew to his chest, tearing at the buttons of his shirt with desperation, wanting to feel him against her *now*. Wanting to feel him inside her now.

Ryan broke off the stimulating kiss, his long fingers curving about her wrists, holding her hands over her head.

"I told you, darlin'," he crooned, "we're in no hurry here. You're behaving like an absolute wanton."

Her body undulated under his warm gaze, an unmistakable invitation as one knee bent unconsciously. "I am," she agreed on a throaty tone. "But only with you, Ryan."

He chuckled, a pleased, self-satisfied masculine sound. "Really?"

"Really, damn you," she complained. "You know you're driving me crazy."

"That's good, sweetheart. Then we'll be on more even footing. Because you've always made me crazy." He gave her a long, lingering kiss that sparked lightning across her brain. "Crazy about you, Brandy Raines."

His fingers were not quite so steady as they unfastened the remaining buttons of her blouse, pulling it from the waistband of her slacks. His lips welcomed every new bit of freed skin, and as her blouse and bra were thrown across the room to land on a chair Ryan gazed down at her.

Her soft tanned skin gleamed golden, lit with a fine sheen of perspiration. His tongue flicked over her experimentally.

"Umm. You taste so good, Brandy. Sweet. So very sweet."

He'd released her hands and now they grasped his neck as she pressed upward toward him.

"Greedy little thing, aren't you?" he said, laughing against her breasts.

"Very greedy," she acknowledged.

"Well then, we'll have to see what we can do to satiate the lady."

Ryan dispatched her slacks with a minimum of effort, pulling them down her legs with a quick, decisive gesture. His thumbs hooked at the waistband of her silky briefs and they, too, soon joined the pile of discarded clothing on the chair.

Brandy expected Ryan to undress, but instead he returned to lie beside her, his lips creating trails of white-hot fire down her body, over her abdomen, his tongue making stabbing forays into her navel that had her crying out with sheer desperation.

"Ryan, please...make love to me."

His lips plucked at the soft skin of her stomach, traveling steadily downward to the juncture of her thighs.

"That's what I'm doing. Just relax and enjoy, honey."

Relax? How in the world did the man expect her to relax when every nerve ending on her body was lit with a burning spark? Any moment she knew she'd be a human inferno.

Her body was limp as he turned her over, his lips and tongue creating the same havoc down her back. Flames licked at her spinal cord, and when his teeth closed on the fleshy part of her anatomy, Brandy could only gasp, words deserting her.

He continued the blazing caresses down the back of her legs, his kisses at the back of her knees causing her to buck against the mattress.

"Please, Ryan...I can't take much more," she begged, wondering even despite her scattered senses about the man's self-control. She felt as if she were on the very brink of a volcano, heat and fire everywhere. Above her, below her and through her.

Ryan turned her onto her back once again, his chestnut head nuzzling against her thighs as his breath warmed the part of her body that had burned for his touch. His lips plucked at the rosy folds, his tongue darting deep within her, and Brandy cried out with a violent, primal sound.

"That's it, honey," he encouraged, his words vibrating against her sensitive core as he failed to slow his assault to her senses. "Don't hold anything back. Let it go."

For thirty years of her life Brandy had maintained an iron control on her emotions. Even with Ryan, she'd kept that slim thread of resistance that had disallowed total surrender. But like dry leaves before a hurricane, all that self-restraint scattered and she arched into his caress, her fists gathering up the sheets at her side.

With all the suicidal tendencies of a moth flinging itself into the flames, she moved against his tormenting touch, her hips surging with an age-old rhythm. Her head was singing with the beat of her own blood and she was infused with a golden heat unlike anything she'd ever known before.

"Oh...Ryan...Ryan!"

His name tore through her body as release came and she shattered in a kaleidoscope of fiery hues—scarlets, golds and amethysts. Duskfire, she realized. She'd just experienced that brilliant death of the sun.

Ryan held her close, seeming to know that while the spiraling ride had been breathtaking, Brandy needed re-assurance on her return to earth. Her breathing was rag-ged, and hot tears poured down her cheeks. But they were not tears of sorrow but of pure, unadulterated joy.

Ryan's lips covered hers in a long, reassuring kiss. She could taste him, warm and familiar. She tasted the salt of the beer he'd had in the Driftwood, and the sweetness of the Scotch he'd been drinking when she'd come out of the bathroom. Her tongue moved experimentally over his lips, delighting in his essence and an unfamiliar tang she knew to be her own.

"I love you, Brandy Raines," he said huskily, his love-darkened eyes shining down at her like a pair of loose emeralds.

"And I love you, Ryan Sinclair," she whispered, her soft expression mirroring his words.

Ryan's face lit up with the glow of a child who'd just seen his first Christmas tree. He rose from the bed, dis-patching his clothes with a speed nothing like the lei-surely undressing he'd submitted her to. When he returned, he settled his long length against her, fitting her curves to his hardness.

"I've wanted to do this since that first moment I saw you coming down the sidewalk, swinging that racket," he murmured into her ear, his teeth nibbling at her del-icate lobe.

"I was a mess," she argued, her hands dancing over his body as she traced the rippling muscles down his back. "Hot, sweaty, my knee was oozing..."

"And all I could think about was lying in bed, both of us naked, you under me like this."

"There are times, Ryan, when I think you have a one-track mind," she teased.

His palms pressed against her inner thighs, spreading them slightly to allow him to move more intimately against her.

"And aren't you glad I do?" he inquired on a growl, uniting them suddenly with a deep thrust.

"Delighted," she gasped, her hands clutching at him, pulling him even farther within her feminine warmth.

Ryan's response was an inarticulate groan as he moved against her, driving her deeper and deeper into the mattress so that she could no longer tell where she left off and the soft foam began. Brandy wrapped her long satiny legs around his hips, marveling that he'd rekindled fires within her that were every bit as hot as those that had scorched her senses earlier.

This time when she was flung into the outer reaches of the universe, Ryan was with her and they clung together, murmuring soft sounds of love.

WHEN BRANDY AWOKE the next morning, her body ached slightly with an unfamiliar stiffness. She stretched like a satisfied tabby cat reclining in the hot sun.

"Beautiful."

She looked over at Ryan, his face lit with an inner glow, his eyes brilliant green gems. "So are you," she said.

"For a writer, your vocabulary definitely needs work. Men are not beautiful."

Her love-softened gaze moved over him. "You are. Absolutely breathtaking."

He laughed. "The woman's crazy, but I love her... Did you get any sleep?"

She grinned impishly. "Some. I seemed to have spent most of the night discovering new erogenous zones. I'm not even going to ask where you learned some of those things, Ryan."

He gave her a teasing leer. "Instinct, sweetheart. All instinct and imagination. That's what we writers are famous for, you know."

She ran her palm down his bare chest, her fingers tangling in the dark pelt.

"That and a few other things," she murmured on a satiny tone.

Ryan muffled a husky groan. "Keep that up and you'll find yourself held prisoner in this bed the rest of the day."

"You can't take prisoners. You're not a cop anymore," she reminded him, her hand inching below the rumpled sheet gathered at his waist.

Ryan reached out and pulled her to him, pressing intimately against her abdomen. "So, I'll make a citizen's arrest."

Her fingers combed through his tousled hair as she tipped her head back, her tawny eyes dancing. "Do you still use handcuffs for things like that?"

His hands moved seductively under the sheet. "Depends. I've always been a pretty straight guy, but I'll try anything that makes you happy, sweetheart."

"You make me happy," she avowed, snuggling closer into his embrace.

"Uh, Brandy?"

"Mmm?"

"I think something's come up between us."

"Mmm," she agreed deliciously, her body rubbing against his like a seductive kitten.

"It's ten o'clock, honey."

"We're writers, Ryan. We don't punch time clocks." Her fingers continued to tease him.

"God, Brandy, you're making this difficult." Even as he objected, Ryan moved against her delicate touch. "Have you forgotten about last night?"

"I haven't forgotten a thing about last night," she murmured, pressing soft kisses against his neck.

Ryan forced his mind from the growing ache in his body to Brandy's problem. "You called your mother last night, honey. She agreed to see you at eleven this morning, remember?"

Her hands flew from him as she flung back the sheet, practically leaping from the bed. How could she have forgotten?

"Oh my God, Ryan, what am I going to do?"

He rose from the bed to stand in front of her, undisturbed by his nudity. Brandy forced her gaze up to his face, wishing she could remain so nonchalant about Ryan Sinclair unclad.

"You'll take a shower in my bathroom, get dressed and go meet your mother... Do you want company on that little social call?"

Brandy wanted Ryan along with her more than she'd ever wanted anything in her life. Including his lovemaking last night. But he'd already done so much for her. This she had to do on her own.

"I'm sorry, Ryan, but..." She faltered, turning away from his loving, encouraging gaze. All he'd done from the beginning was give. And all she'd done was take, offering nothing in return. Brandy Raines had never before considered herself a selfish individual, and it was an unpleasant revelation.

"Hey, I understand."

She looked back over her shoulder. "Why are you so good to me?"

He shrugged. "I'm in love with you," he said simply. "Now go get ready. I'll have some coffee waiting for you. Then you can take my car and I'll be waiting here when you get back."

He was amazing. "How long will you wait?" she asked softly.

His emerald gaze held hers. "As long as it takes."

"I don't deserve you," she whispered.

An angry flush darkened his face as Ryan began yanking on his clothes.

"We've been through that before, Brandy. The one thing I won't stand for is you putting yourself down. Understand?" His eyes burned into hers like green lasers.

"Understand," she murmured, feeling like a crab scuttling away in the sand as she left the room.

"YOU LOOK GREAT," Ryan said as he handed her a cup of steaming coffee.

"I feel awful. You know the old saying about butterflies in the stomach?"

He nodded.

"Well, I've got giant condors, Ryan."

"Hey, you'll do fine, kid."

She walked over to the window, looking down at the white-foamed surf. "What if she doesn't like me?"

He remained where he was. Ryan wanted to cross the large room, gather her into his arms, rain kisses all over her distressed face and promise never to let anything or anyone hurt her again. But he could see she was struggling to maintain control of her emotions and decided that physical contact between them at this point would be playing with dynamite.

"I can't imagine anyone not liking you, honey," he said honestly.

"She didn't like me when I was born."

Ryan stifled the muffled curse, realizing Brandy was only seeking reassurance. He tried to give it to her.

"Brandy, Jake explained all that. She was seventeen years old, she was dating a sailor who sailed out of San Diego without ever knowing he had fathered a child, and she was all alone."

"She wouldn't have been alone if she'd kept me," she argued irrationally.

He expelled a soft breath of frustration. "Look, honey, the day Marianne Baxter put you in that patrol car she had been out of work for two months and had just been evicted. As far as she was concerned, she'd just run out of options."

"But when she came back to ask about me, Jake gave her a job. Why didn't she try to get me back then?"

"And raise you in that room she was living in over the Driftwood? Come on, Brandy, what kind of life would that have been?"

"I'd have at least had a family of sorts. A mother. Jake. Even L.J. Someone to love me."

"I love you."

She spun toward him, her entire body trembling with emotion. "That's not the same, damn it!"

Ryan's eyes were shuttered. "Why isn't it?"

"Because it's based on sex. It's not the love family members have for each other."

His voice was deadly calm. "Are you telling me that the love I have for Kevin is somehow more *noble* than the love I have for you?"

"Noble's not the right word," she argued weakly.

"Well then, since you're such a renowned writer of emotions, Brandy Raines, why don't you explain to me which term defines these feelings." His tone was full of sarcasm.

"I don't know, damn it!" Brandy shrieked at him, realizing that while the difference had always seemed clear in her mind, right now the lines had blurred and he had her confused. "You're the one with the big family, Ryan. You should understand what I'm trying to say."

"I only understand that you're way off base, Brandy. And if you're that unwilling to admit to what we've got, I don't know that anything I can do or say will make this work."

He dug into his pockets, pulling out his car keys. He threw them to her in a wide, looping toss. "You'd better get going. I'd hate to stand in the way of true love."

He left the room, slamming the door of the den. Brandy stared after him for a long, silent time. Then she went out to the car, grinding through the gears as she roared down the roadway.

Brandy forced herself to remain calm as she drove up the coast to Oceanside, where her mother was living with her husband, a Marine sergeant stationed at Camp Pendleton.

As she parked the car and walked up to the small frame house, she felt her knees shaking and wished suddenly that Ryan was with her. If nothing else, at least he could hold her up.

The woman who answered the door appeared a little hesitant herself, and for a long, silent moment the two stared at each other, both pairs of tawny eyes making appraisal.

Marianne Baxter was not as tall as Brandy, but her figure was just as slender. Her hair was a darker honey, with strands of silver woven through it, as if she'd decided, at forty-seven, to allow nature to take its course. Her eyes were the giveaway. Soft, and of a golden amber hue, they mirrored Brandy's. Her full lips offered a tentative smile.

"Won't you come in?" she asked politely. "I've made us some tea."

"Thank you," Brandy answered just as formally.

As she was led into a small living room, Brandy's attention was drawn to a trophy rack hanging on the wall.

"Those are Jason's," Marianne offered, following Brandy's gaze.

"Jason?"

She nodded, gesturing for Brandy to take a seat on the sofa. "My son. He bowls very well. In fact, he's thinking of turning pro."

"Oh." Brandy sat down, her mind whirling. She had a brother who bowled. Her family was growing by leaps and bounds.

"Jason's my oldest. Then there's Todd, who just turned sixteen two weeks ago. We haven't seen too much of him since he got his driver's license."

Marianne smiled fondly at the thought of her son, and Brandy tried not to be hurt by the fact that she'd described Jason Baxter as her eldest child, as if Brandy had never existed.

"Amy is fourteen and spoiled rotten. But she's so pretty that everyone lets her get away with murder." Marianne's eyes skimmed over Brandy. "Actually, she looks a great deal like you. Would you like to see a picture?"

"That would be nice," Brandy answered politely, half curious and half jealous of these individuals who had grown up with this woman as their mother.

Marianne excused herself and Brandy took advantage of her absence to study the homey room. She attempted to picture herself as a child, stacking blocks on the oak floor, but failed miserably. *Try something a little older,* she instructed her well-honed imagination. She stared at the stairway, attempting to picture a teenage girl running down the stairs, her cheerleader's skirt swirling about her legs as she breathlessly explained to a patient, smiling mother that she simply didn't have time to eat before the big game.

Strike two, she thought with a sigh as the image failed to materialize. At that moment Marianne returned, carrying a large photo album.

"This is Amy," she said, sitting beside Brandy and opening to a photograph of a smiling girl, her wide teeth encased in braces.

"She wears braces," Brandy said softly, more to herself than Marianne.

"And hates them," Marianne revealed. "I swear, the day she came home from the orthodontist she locked herself in her bedroom and cried for hours. She didn't want anyone to see her with 'a metal mouth' as she calls it."

"It's better than having them stick out so far they enter a room before you," Brandy observed, remembering her own torturous teenage years.

She'd learned to talk without moving her lips and never laughed for fear of showing her crooked, protruding teeth. Once Billy Lambert had tried to kiss her in the back hallway and had given up, saying it was far too dangerous. He'd spread the story and Brandy Raines's lethal mouth had been the laughingstock of the school for weeks.

"That's what we tried to tell her, but you know how vain teenage girls are," Marianne replied with a cheerful shake of her head. "She's only just forgiven me for handing down my crooked teeth. You were lucky, Brandy; yours are perfect."

"Lucky," Brandy murmured.

"So you're a writer."

"Yes."

"That's very impressive. Romances, right?"

Brandy nodded. "That's right. Although I just finished working on a romantic suspense with a collaborator."

"Ryan Sinclair," Marianne filled in. At Brandy's surprised glance, she elaborated. "Jake told me. I'd love to tell John—he's my husband—but I can't figure out any way to casually mention that I know someone who knows Ryan Sinclair. John absolutely adored *The Killing Hour*. And he stayed up all night reading *The Uninvited Corpse*."

"Couldn't you tell him the truth?" Brandy ventured hesitantly.

"Oh, no," Marianne answered quickly. A little too quickly. She had the grace to blush as she avoided Brandy's gaze. "You see, Brandy, John doesn't know anything about you. I never got around to telling him, and it's a little late now."

It's too late, Brandy agreed silently.

"Why don't you bring the album into the kitchen and we'll talk while we have lunch," Marianne suggested, pasting an encouraging smile on her face.

"That's not necessary," Brandy demurred, suddenly wanting to go back home. Back to Ryan.

"Of course it is," the elder woman insisted firmly. "You must have at least a few questions."

Over bacon-and-tomato sandwiches, Marianne answered all Brandy's questions, assuring her there was nothing in either family that would discourage her from having children. As if offering proof, Marianne turned to page after page in the family album, showing Brandy candid photos of her family, all three Baxter children exhibiting exuberant health.

These are my half sister and half brothers, Brandy thought to herself, wondering why she felt no tug of recognition. No fulfilling flow of familial love. It was also a shock to discover that she felt no emotion whatsoever toward the woman seated across the table from her.

"I don't suppose you have any pictures of me, when I was a baby?" she asked tentatively.

Marianne's eyes shadowed. "No, I'm afraid not."

Strike three. Brandy accepted the fact that her dreams of finding her parents and living happily ever after had been built on foundations of fantasy. Marianne Baxter was friendly, helpful and very nice. But she could have been a stranger.

"I think I'd better be going," Brandy said finally.

Marianne cast a quick glance at the sunshine-yellow kitchen clock. "That's probably best. Amy will be home soon, and there's always the chance she might recognize the resemblance." Her expression revealed her discomfort. "I hope you understand why I can't tell my family about you, Brandy. I was young and an entirely different person from the woman they all know. The adjustment would be extremely difficult for everyone involved."

"I understand," Brandy murmured, rising from the table.

"Oh, wait a minute—I almost forgot!" Marianne ran from the room, returning with a copy of *Love's Savage Embrace*. "Would you autograph this for me?"

Brandy felt a surge of pleasure that her mother had actually read her book. "Of course," she agreed instantly. "Did you enjoy it?"

"Well, to tell you the truth, I only bought it this morning. I don't read very much. I never seem to have the time."

"Oh. Jason, Todd and Amy must keep you very busy."

The dry tone flew right over Marianne Baxter's head. "They do," she affirmed. "But I wouldn't trade them for the world." Suddenly realizing what she'd said, Marianne's face darkened with a guilty flush.

"That's all right," Brandy assured her. "I understand." And she did, she realized suddenly. She opened the book, taking the pen Marianne offered. The point poised over the page as she tried to think of something suitable to write.

"Why don't you put, 'To my friend, Marianne. With best wishes'?" Marianne suggested.

Brandy signed the page with a flourish, handing the unread novel back to her mother, who looked inordinately pleased.

"Thank you, dear," she said, walking Brandy to the door. "Now tell me that you'll come visit again soon."

"I will," Brandy agreed, knowing as she said the words that she'd never return. She realized Marianne knew it, too, as the woman gave her a quick, almost nervous peck on the cheek before closing the door.

"She was a stranger," Brandy murmured to herself as she drove slowly along the Coast Highway, choosing the longer route to allow her time to sort out her feelings. "I felt more kinship at Kevin's birthday party than I did in that house today."

As she returned to La Jolla, to that magnificent seaside home, and Ryan, Brandy began to understand what Ryan had been trying to tell her all along.

Love was not something granted automatically, passed down from generation to generation like a family heirloom. It was born of individuals willing to trust in one another, sharing the good times as well as the bad and working together to ensure their love will thrive in an imperfect world.

Ryan had given her more love and understanding in their weeks together than she'd received her entire life. And while she bore no animosity toward her mother, neither had she felt that instant love and recognition she'd always believed blood ties would bring. Brandy sighed, aware of a bittersweet regret for all the years she'd wasted, waiting for this day.

Ryan flung open the door as she pulled the Porsche into the driveway, but remained standing where he was. Tentative green eyes scanned her face as she walked toward him, searching for a hint as to her mood.

"How did it go?" he asked.

Brandy nodded. "Fine. As fine as can be expected."

His expression revealed nothing. "Did you find what you've been looking for then?"

She nodded again.

"I'm happy for you, Brandy. Honestly I am."

She reached up, putting her arms around his neck. "I found the man I love and want to spend the rest of my life with," she murmured.

Ryan's eyes exploded with golden fireworks. "Do you mean...?"

"I've come home," she said simply.

Ryan needed no further invitation. He scooped her easily into his arms, carrying her through the house into the bedroom. As they made love, this time was different from the others in that Brandy was pledging an eternal commitment with every touch. Every kiss.

"WHAT ARE WE GOING TO DO about a house?" he asked. "We seem to have two."

"We could always save mine for weekends," she suggested. "It's nice and quiet up there. And in the autumn they have the apple festival...."

"You wouldn't mind moving in here?"

Brandy grinned. "Not as long as I'm allowed to buy some furniture. This place is like a warehouse, Ryan. A magnificent, empty warehouse."

"You can fill it with whatever you want, honey. The money we're going to make collaborating should pay for any little thing your heart desires."

Her fingers played in the lush carpeting of chest hair. "How about filling it with children?"

Ryan's hand covered hers, and Brandy could feel the sudden increase of his heartbeat against her palm.

"Are you serious?"

She pressed a long delicious kiss against his lips. "Of course. And now that I've decided to make my own family, I think I'll keep you tied to this bed until you deliver."

His eyes sparkled at her teasing insinuation. "My handcuffs are in the top dresser drawer."

She covered his hard body with her own, wiggling seductively. "Will I need restraints?"

He lifted her hips, settling her down onto him and Brandy caught her breath at the burst of pleasure their union created. She loved him. Freely and openly and forever.

"Only to keep me tied down to that word processor once in a while so we can afford to feed the little Sinclairs." He laughed huskily. "I think writing has become my second favorite thing to do."

"We do write well together, don't we Ryan?" Brandy asked on a breathless note as his roving hands did warm and wonderful things to her body.

"We do everything well together, my love." His lips plucked enticingly at hers.

Her mind was spinning away at warp speed from any discussion of work, but there was one question she'd been dying to ask him for weeks. Brandy struggled to maintain a grip on her senses just long enough to learn the answer.

"Are you going to continue writing about Johnny Steele?"

His teeth closed on her earlobe, tugging gently. "Do you want me to?" he asked, knowing her feelings about his rather seedy detective.

Brandy surprised him. "I've come to appreciate certain aspects of his personality." Her hips moved in seductive circles, "waving a happy hello," Ryan thought irreverently.

"Then I'll do my best to keep the old reprobate around," he promised, his movements answering hers with increased eroticism. "But those Steele books are going to be a helluva lot harder to write than they used to be, I'm afraid."

"Why?"

Ryan thrust upward, the rigid strength of his body demonstrating that he was ready to put away this conversation. He tangled his fingers in her hair, pulling her head down for a long kiss.

"Because, since meeting a certain seductive romance writer," he admitted on a husky note, before turning to matters far more inviting, "I've found I'm a sucker for the happy ending."

You're invited to accept 4 books and a surprise gift Free!

Acceptance Card

Mail to: **Harlequin Reader Service®**

In the U.S.
2504 West Southern Ave.
Tempe, AZ 85282

In Canada
P.O. Box 2800, Postal Station A
5170 Yonge Street
Willowdale, Ontario M2N 6J3

YES! Please send me 4 free Harlequin Temptation® novels and my free surprise gift. Then send me 4 brand new novels every month as they come off the presses. Bill me at the low price of $1.99 each ($1.95 in Canada)—a 13% saving off the retail price. There are no shipping, handling or other hidden costs. There is no minimum number of books I must purchase. I can always return a shipment and cancel at any time. Even if I never buy another book from Harlequin, the 4 free novels and the surprise gift are mine to keep forever.

142 BPX-BPGE

Name _____ (PLEASE PRINT)

Address _____ Apt. No. _____

City _____ State/Prov. _____ Zip/Postal Code _____

This offer is limited to one order per household and not valid to present subscribers. Price is subject to change.

ACHT-SUB-1

H·A·R·L·E·Q·U·I·N

FIRST·CLASS
Sweepstakes

OFFICIAL RULES

1. NO PURCHASE NECESSARY. To enter, complete the official entry/order form. Be sure to indicate whether or not you wish to take advantage of our subscription offer.

2. Entry blanks have been preselected for the prizes offered. Your response will be checked to see if you are a winner. In the event that these preselected responses are not claimed, a random drawing will be held from all entries received to award not less than $150,000 in prizes. This is in addition to any free, surprise or mystery gifts which might be offered. Versions of this sweepstakes with different prizes will appear in Preview Service Mailings by Harlequin Books and their affiliates. Winners selected will receive the prize offered in their sweepstakes brochure.

3. This promotion is being conducted under the supervision of Marden-Kane, an independent judging organization. By entering the sweepstakes, each entrant accepts and agrees to be bound by these rules and the decisions of the judges, which shall be final and binding. Odds of winning in the random drawing are dependent upon the total number of entries received. Taxes, if any, are the sole responsibility of the prize winners. Prizes are nontransferable. All entries must be received by August 31, 1986.

4. The following prizes will be awarded:

   (1) Grand Prize: Rolls-Royce™ *or* $100,000 Cash!
   (Rolls-Royce being offered by permission of Rolls-Royce Motors Inc.)

   (1) Second Prize: A trip for two to Paris for 7 days/6 nights. Trip includes air transportation on the Concorde, hotel accommodations...PLUS...$5,000 spending money!

   (1) Third Prize: A luxurious Mink Coat!

5. This offer is open to residents of the U.S. and Canada, 18 years or older, except employees of Harlequin Books, its affiliates, subsidiaries, Marden-Kane and all other agencies and persons connected with conducting this sweepstakes. All Federal, State and local laws apply. Void in the province of Quebec and wherever prohibited or restricted by law. Winners will be notified by mail and may be required to execute an affidavit of eligibility and release, which must be returned within 14 days after notification. Canadian winners will be required to answer a skill-testing question. Winners consent to the use of their name, photograph and/or likeness for advertising and publicity purposes in conjunction with this and similar promotions without additional compensation. One prize per family or household.

6. For a list of our most current prize winners, send a stamped, self-addressed envelope to: WINNERS LIST, c/o Marden-Kane, P.O. Box 10404, Long Island City, New York 11101